Multn
Title W
D0199722
216 NE Knott St, Portland, OR
503-988-5021

INSPIRED BY ACTUAL EVENTS

STANDING STRONG

Gary Robinson

7th GENERATION
Summertown, Tennessee

Library of Congress Cataloging-in-Publication Data

Names: Robinson, Gary, 1950- author.
Title: Standing strong / Gary Robinson.
Description: Summertown, Tennessee : 7th Generation, [2019] | "Inspired by Actual Events." | Summary: After a failed suicide attempt, seventeen-year-old Rhonda Runningcrane is inspired to help a crew protesting against an oil company running a pipeline through sacred Native land in North Dakota.
Identifiers: LCCN 2019002633 (print) | LCCN 2019005423 (ebook) | ISBN 9781939053770 (ebook) | ISBN 9781939053220 (pbk.)
Subjects: | CYAC: Protest movements—Fiction. | Suicidal behavior—Fiction. | Siksika Indians—Fiction. | Indians of North America—Montana—Fiction. | Standing Rock Indian Reservation (N.D. and S.D.)—Fiction. | Montana--Fiction. | North Dakota—Fiction.
Classification: LCC PZ7.R56577 (ebook) | LCC PZ7.R56577 St 2019 (print) | DDC [Fic]—dc23
LC record available at https://lccn.loc.gov/2019002633

© 2019 Gary Robinson

Cover and interior design: John Wincek

All rights reserved. No portion of this book may be reproduced by any means whatsoever, except for brief quotations in reviews, without written permission from the publisher.

7th Generation
Book Publishing Company
PO Box 99, Summertown, TN 38483
888-260-8458
bookpubco.com
nativevoicesbooks.com

ISBN: 978-1-939053-22-0

24 23 22 21 20 19 1 2 3 4 5 6 7 8 9

CONTENTS

This book is dedicated to two different groups of people. First are the Water Protectors at the Standing Rock Indian Reservation who provided the inspiration for this story, along with all the Native and non-Native people who continue to work to protect our natural sources of water from contamination by oil spills, pipeline leaks, and other man-made environmental disasters.

Water Protectors come from all walks of life and carry out their protective duties in different ways. Some are attorneys who take the fight to protect our water into the courts. Others, such as the Water Protectors in this story, drop everything else in their lives to camp out for weeks or months at a time at a pipeline protest site.

Second are the Native American teen suicide survivors, like the main character in *Standing Strong*. My hope for these young people is for them to engage in the issues and situations that may have led to their attempt. May they learn all they can about the causes of negative social conditions that surround them and work toward healing themselves and their communities. Every person has value, and the world is a better place with each of them in it.

Where Did the Happiness Go?

The sun was setting beyond the Backbone of the World, the Rocky Mountain Range that ran along the western edge of the Blackfeet Reservation. Rhonda Runningcrane, a red bandana keeping her long brown hair tied back, was finishing up a carburetor she was adjusting in her uncle Floyd's repair shop in downtown Browning, Montana.

"Got any plans for the summer?" Floyd, a fairly fit Native man in his mid-forties, asked as he rolled out from under the 1985 Chevy pickup he'd just finished working on. "A tour of Europe? A cruise of the Pacific?"

"Ha-ha. Very funny," Rhonda replied. "More like working the graveyard shift at the Towne Pump convenience store to earn some money."

"You know you could earn some cash helping me a few hours a week," her uncle said. "Fixing cars, repairing houses, chopping wood for elders—the kind of stuff you and I have been doing ever since you were little."

"How could you afford to pay me anything?" she asked. "You don't even charge for half the work you do for people on this rez."

"My veterans disability checks keep me in fry bread and beans," he replied. "My mobile home is paid for, so I don't need much else."

He wiped his hands on a shop rag and opened the driver's side door of the truck.

"Let's take her for a test drive. I need to run out to the house and check on that sick mare."

He gestured for her to slide into the driver's seat, and the seventeen-year-old climbed in behind the wheel. Rhonda knew the way to her uncle's place like she knew the back of her hand. His little mini-ranch sitting next to Cut Bank Creek had been a place of refuge since she was a kid.

Rhonda's uncle Floyd, her mother's brother, had often taken up the slack when the girl's own mother and father had failed her as parents. Rhonda knew what he was up to now, trying to keep her busy so she wouldn't have time for suicidal thoughts or bouts of depression.

Back in March, Rhonda had attempted suicide. There's no way to sugarcoat it or pretend it didn't happen. Truth is, she and her best friend, Claudia, had made a pact, an agreement, to kill themselves. Actually, they weren't the only ones in on the pact. A few other Native teens at their high school had also made a vow to end their own lives.

Understanding how or why they all came to such a desperate decision is nearly impossible unless you've been there, done that, so to speak. Their main goal was to escape. Escape the dead-end feelings they all shared. Escape what they considered to be a hopeless situation. Escape any way you could. They dared one another to do it.

The thing is, Claudia succeeded in her suicide attempt, whereas Rhonda had failed. In her own mind, Rhonda added this failure to the long list of failures in her life. Claudia's life ended just three days ago, so Rhonda's own feelings were rather raw.

Rhonda now drove the stick-shift Chevy pickup north on Boundary Road about three miles, then turned northeast onto the asphalt-topped Boarding School Road. The darkening, late-May sky hovered overhead like a smothering mother bear clinging too tightly to her cubs. At least that's how it felt to Rhonda.

"How are you and your grandmother getting along?" Floyd asked from the passenger seat. "Any improvement on the home front?"

Last year, the Blackfeet Tribal Court awarded custody of Rhonda to her father's mother, Geraldine Runningcrane, in spite of the objections of Rhonda's legal representative. Rhonda's lawyer argued that Geraldine was verbally and physically abusive, and the elderly woman's aging frame house was an unsafe residence. Rhonda lost that court battle.

"The old woman is meaner than ever," Rhonda said. "Why the court awarded custody to her instead of you, I still don't understand."

"Like the judge said, it wouldn't look right for a teen girl to be staying with an unmarried older uncle," Floyd answered in a quiet, firm voice. "Especially after Claudia's uncle molested her right before she killed herself."

"But you are nothing like Claudia's uncle," Rhonda protested. "Everybody knows that."

"But, later on, if something like that happened to you, the judge could be held responsible for not properly protecting teen girls here on the rez," Floyd explained. "The court thinks of a grandmother as a closer relative than an uncle."

Seeing that the topic brought back anger and frustration to his niece, Floyd shrugged and just said, "It is what it is."

They rode in silence for a moment.

"I added a little solar-powered light to the top of the fence post to make the gate easier to see at night," he said as they approached the turnoff to his property in the growing darkness. "It stores up power during the day. There it is up ahead."

Rhonda slowed the truck and made the left turn onto the gravel road leading to Floyd's place. When she pulled up to the gate, Floyd jumped down and opened it. After the truck passed through, he closed the gate and climbed back into the truck's cab.

Just then, Rhonda's cell phone rang. Looking at the phone's screen, she saw the caller was her grandmother. She swiped downward on the screen to let the call go to voicemail. A few moments later, Floyd's phone rang. This call was also from Rhonda's grandmother. He took the call, much to his niece's disappointment, and turned on the speaker.

"Hello, Geraldine," he said politely. "How are you this fine Blackfeet evening?"

"Cut the crap, Floyd," Rhonda's grandmother said angrily. Her speech was slightly slurred from the effects of alcohol. "You and Rhonda both know she's supposed to be home by dark! Court orders. Send her home right now!"

"She's probably hanging out with her friends, but if I see her, I'll tell her to get on home," he assured her, giving Rhonda a sly little smile. "You better believe it."

"I don't believe anything you say, mister," Geraldine barked. "She's probably right there listening to me! Rhonda, you'd better get your butt home quick. I swear I'll call the tribal cops on your uncle. I'll tell 'em he's a pedophile."

"All right then, Geraldine," Floyd replied as he tried to maintain a polite tone of voice. "You have yourself a good evening."

He ended the call and looked at his niece.

"She sounds pissed," Rhonda said. "As usual."

"I'm sorry, Rhonda, but I'd better get you home," Floyd said. "Knowing her, she *will* call the cops on me and make up some kind of false accusation."

"Okay. If you say so," she said, accepting her fate. "You drive."

They switched seats, and Floyd steered the truck southward toward the Blackfeet housing development where Rhonda's grandmother lived. Meanwhile, Rhonda escaped into the social media world provided by her cell phone as they passed through the pitted streets of the capital of the Blackfeet Nation.

In a few minutes, the truck came to a stop in front of a gray, wood-frame house that looked like every other wood-frame house in the tribal neighborhood. A dying tree and a yard full of unmowed grass greeted them at the curb.

Knowing what waited for her inside that house, Rhonda wordlessly exited the truck and briskly walked away. Floyd watched her open the door and go inside.

"Dammit, girl, get in here and fix my dinner!" were the words Rhonda's grandmother hurled at her before the door had even closed behind the teen.

The thin, elderly Native woman held a glass of iced whiskey in one hand and a cigarette in the other.

"You know this diabetes could kill me if I go too long without food!" she added.

Rhonda rushed past her and headed straight for the kitchen. Geraldine followed her granddaughter into the room as the girl opened the freezer and withdrew two frozen dinners.

"You need to spend more time here with me instead of doing God-knows-what with your worthless friends or that loser uncle of yours," the woman advised. "It'll be my rear end they come after if you get in trouble or try to off yourself again."

"You're so kind and understanding," Rhonda said sarcastically. "No wonder my father drank and took drugs!"

"Your father took drugs because that worthless woman he married, your mother, got him hooked on the stuff," Geraldine said angrily. "My son is dead because of her!"

It was true that Rhonda's mother had killed her father just over a year ago. But it wasn't true that Rhonda's mother got her father hooked on drugs. Rhonda's father had become an abusive alcoholic, and he beat her mother on a regular basis. When the woman finally had enough, she fought back, killing the man in self-defense. The judge sent to her to jail anyway.

Standing in the kitchen, Rhonda was about to sling insults back at her grandmother when she remembered what her therapist said about not escalating a pointless argument. She took a couple of deep breaths, calmed herself, and decided not to engage in the fight about her parents one more time.

"What you told Uncle Floyd on the phone isn't true anymore," she said calmly. "My court-ordered curfew ended two days ago when my high school classes finished, so I can stay out as late as I want to with whoever I want to."

"The days of no curfew don't start until you officially graduate," the elderly woman snarled. "That's not until Saturday, but you'll do as I say as long as you live under my roof!"

"That'll end, too, in a month and a half when I turn eighteen," the girl replied as she placed the two frozen trays of food in the microwave. She turned to face her grandmother.

"You want to know the real reason I tried to kill myself?" Rhonda said sharply, not waiting for an answer. "Because death has to be better than this hell I'm living here with you!"

With that, she stormed out of the kitchen, ran down the hall, and locked herself in her room. Overcome with a deep sadness, she flung herself on her unmade bed. Tears flowed freely as she hugged her pillow tightly. In a few moments, her sobbing subsided, and she reached for a tattered photo on her nightstand.

Wiping the tears away, she gazed at the image of her ten-year-old self, standing between her mother and father. The three smiling faces were the only evidence that Rhonda had once known happiness. Where did that happiness go? What happened to that bright, promising world?

Her phone pinged, and she put the photo down. So what if her therapist had recommended not spending so much time on Instagram and Facebook. Sure, the electronic world is filled with allies and bullies, friends and foes, just like the real world. But at least there, no one could physically harm you.

Spending time online also kept Rhonda from spiraling downward within her own thoughts. To prevent this, her therapist wanted her to do something called journaling. Rhonda tried it a couple of times, but she couldn't keep from just writing down her negative opinions and attitudes.

In her first journaling effort, she wrote, "*Where do I start? So much has happened in my seventeen, almost eighteen years living on this reservation, and yet it seems like absolutely nothing has happened. Nothing has changed. I'm standing still. The Indians on this rez are just a bunch of broken-down, dysfunctional people with nothing to look forward to, nothing to live for. We've been beat to the bone and left for dead.*"

It was then she remembered it was that kind of thinking that got her to where she was these days—the survivor of attempted suicide. What a cliché she was: another Native teen making the attempt. Those thoughts reminded her about tomorrow. Claudia's funeral. Two days after that would come high school graduation.

Rhonda's therapist said it was important to set goals, work to achieve them, and celebrate when you accomplish them. "So," Rhonda thought, "I'm graduating from high school—big frickin' deal. It's not like that's going to get me anywhere. Oops.

There are those negative thoughts again. I just can't seem to escape them."

Therapy sessions began while Rhonda was still in the hospital recovering from her "attempt," as they called it. For the first few days, the woman therapist would show up in the girl's room, and for those first few days, the teen refused to talk to the woman. But the therapist kept coming, bringing little "bribes" of food that tasted far better than anything the hospital kitchen made.

The therapist began reading a young-adult novel out loud about a girl in Seattle who'd attempted suicide and failed. The girl in the book had avoided confrontation all her life and had always found ways to escape from uncomfortable situations. She couldn't face her fears or deal with her troubles—just like Rhonda.

Without sounding judgmental or preachy, the therapist began to reach beyond Rhonda's tough exterior into her wounded inner self, the little girl who had been scared all her life. That's when Rhonda began to really listen and respond to her therapy sessions. She realized her challenge was to begin valuing herself and confronting obstacles.

The therapist said it would be a long road to reach that goal, but it would never happen without taking the first steps.

Saying Goodbye

Saturday morning came, and Rhonda did not want to attend her best friend's funeral even though they had promised one another. Whichever one died first, the other one swore to go to watch how people reacted and to say a public goodbye to her friend.

But there would be awkward stares and hushed whispers to deal with. Of course, everyone knew Rhonda had tried it first. But no one knew about the secret suicide pact she had made with Claudia and the other teens.

Rhonda clawed through the clothes in her closet looking for something to wear. She wasn't a frilly girl, and she didn't own any church clothes. No one in her family had ever gone to church except for weddings and funerals. Too much self-righteous judgment and condemnation.

Finally, she settled on a reasonably clean Grateful Dead T-shirt that had belonged to her mother and a pair of only slightly wrinkled jeans. Her therapist had said that going to the funeral for her own mental health was more important than what she wore.

Thankfully, her grandmother was sleeping off another hangover, so Rhonda got out of the house without an unpleasant confrontation. As she walked the few blocks to the Four Winds Baptist Church, the teen thought about one of the good times she'd had with Claudia.

They were under the bleachers at a high school baseball game sharing a joint with a couple of other friends. Of course, smoking marijuana on campus was against all the rules. But who cared? Certainly not Rhonda and her friends. They'd heard about all the dangers of pot use in their health class and that about half of all Native kids in the U.S. had tried it or some other drug.

Anyway, the four of them were pretty wasted by the time they were discovered by a teacher. As the older white man headed for them at a brisk pace, Claudia yelled, "Custer!" That was their prearranged signal to split up and head in four different directions. The teacher was so confused that he didn't know which way to go or who to follow. So he just stood there with a dazed look, and all four of them got away.

That memory brought a smile to Rhonda's face as she turned down the sidewalk that led to the front of the church. She could hear that familiar and depressing organ music spilling out from the open double doors. A few other stragglers like her made their way inside to find seats in the back of the unadorned sanctuary.

As she scanned the pews, Rhonda's phone pinged, telling her she had a new text. It was from Nadie, one of her best under-the-bleacher buddies.

"*In the back right corner*," the text read. "*Saved you a seat*."

Rhonda looked in that direction and found her friend in a back row. Sitting next to her was her other favorite rule-breaker, Koko. Nadie patted the empty pew seat beside her as the preacher started the service.

"Dearly beloved friends," Reverend Wolftail began as Rhonda took her seat. "It's another sad day here on the reservation as we gather on another mournful occasion."

The rotund Native man was well known on the rez for his hellfire and brimstone preaching style. Rhonda and her friends found it particularly annoying.

"But I am not going to sugarcoat it," he bellowed. "I'm going to get right to it. The book of Hebrews tells us it is appointed for a man to die once, and after that comes judgment. Can I get an amen?"

Several people in the audience complied by shouting, "Amen!"

The reverend continued.

"The book of First Corinthians tells us, 'Do you not know that you are God's temple and that God's spirit dwells in you? If anyone destroys God's temple, God will destroy him.'"

And so it began. The judgment and condemnation Rhonda had expected was right up front. She immediately tuned the man out and began texting with Nadie and Koko, although the pair sat right beside her.

The service seemed to go on forever, but when it was finally over, the reverend parked himself just outside the front doors of the church. There he greeted all who passed by, shaking their hands and offering a few words of comfort. Hoping to avoid an encounter with him, Rhonda and her friends tried to slip by while the man was talking to one of his regulars.

"Excuse me, young lady. Could I have a word with you?" Wolftail asked, looking right at Rhonda.

The girl looked around to see if maybe he could be referring to someone else.

"Yes, I'm talking to you, Rhonda," he said as he stepped closer to the three girls.

"Okay. I guess so," Rhonda replied reluctantly.

"I know you're not a member of my congregation, but for some reason, God has laid it on my heart to give you a message," he said.

"A message?" she asked, fearing it was some kind of evangelical trick. "What kind of message?"

"Just this," he answered. "Your best means of escape is to take on a cause bigger than yourself, somewhere beyond this place, where you can channel your energy to protect someone or something that needs your help."

Coming out of nowhere, this message took Rhonda completely by surprise. She pondered the preacher's words for a moment, not knowing what to make of the message. The reverend remained silent, apparently not knowing himself what to make of the unusual message he was delivering.

"I don't know exactly what this means or what that cause might be," he finally said. "But I trust God to know what it is, and I hope you'll recognize it when you find it."

With that, he excused himself and walked back inside the church, leaving a long line of puzzled and disappointed mourners who were still waiting to shake his hand.

"What was that?" Nadie asked. "What just happened?

"I don't know," Rhonda said, "but it totally creeps me out."

"Yeah, me, too," Koko said. "Let's get out of here. My car's across the street."

Koko drove them westward a few blocks to one of their usual hangouts, the North American Indian Days Campground. During the second weekend in July, the place would be a beehive of activity with hundreds of dancers and their families camped out in countless numbers of tipis and tents pitched for the annual weekend of powwow dances and other events.

The rest of the year, the place was mostly an empty plot of ground patterned with dirt paths and circles in the grass left by the tipis. In the center of it all was the round powwow dance arbor. The middle of the area was open to the sky, but the circular rows of stadium seating facing the middle were covered with a tin roof.

Koko drove her car to the edge of the dance arbor and parked it. Nadie and Rhonda got out while Koko searched for the joint she'd stored in the glove compartment earlier. Finding it, she looked around to make sure no one was watching. Carrying the joint and a lighter, she joined the girls on the upper back row of the stadium-style seating.

"I think that preacher must've been smoking something himself," Rhonda said as she took a hit from the joint. "I've never heard anything like that before."

"He was right about one thing," Nadie said. "We gotta escape one way or another."

"What do you think he meant about taking on a cause bigger than yourself or protecting someone?" Koko asked.

"No clue," Rhonda replied. "I'm no protector of anything. I can't even take care of myself, let alone anyone else."

They continued chatting and smoking for a while. Then Nadie, who had been a Fancy Shawl Dancer when she was younger, got up and started moving around inside the arena. Stepping to a drumbeat only she could hear, the girl began dancing as if she was wearing a Fancy Shawl outfit. Her arm movements made her look a little like a butterfly.

Seeing what her friend was doing, Koko began drumming on the aluminum bench seat beside her. The sound echoed across the open space, inspiring Nadie to intensify her dance steps.

Not wanting to be left out, Rhonda joined in the little pretend scenario by mimicking a powwow announcer.

"Ladies and gentlemen, boys and girls!" she shouted, pretending her cell phone was a microphone. "Put your hands together to show your appreciation for the dance stylings of Ms. Nadie Buffalo Child!" She clapped her hands and yelled, "And the crowd goes wild!"

Lost in their little fantasy, none of the girls noticed when a tribal police car pulled into the dance arena. Dressed in blue, a Native female officer stepped out of the vehicle and approached the girls.

"You know you girls aren't supposed to be here," the officer said in a loud voice.

The girls froze and looked at the cop. Luckily, they had finished smoking their joint.

Rhonda recognized the Native woman. Using her most innocent voice, Rhonda said, "Sorry, Officer Weatherwax. We aren't hurting anyone."

The cop sniffed the air.

"Have you been smoking marijuana?" she asked as she stepped closer to Rhonda. "Empty your pockets on the bench over there."

Following orders, the girls pulled sticks of gum, cell phones, car keys, a little cash, and other stuff from their various pockets.

Finding nothing incriminating, the officer said, "Okay, you can return the items to your pockets."

The girls quickly did so.

"Someone has been vandalizing this area during the past few weeks," Weatherwax said. "So we're keeping an eye on things to prevent further damage.

You girls move along quick now, or I might have to take you in for questioning."

"Yes, ma'am," Koko said in a falsely polite tone. "Right away, ma'am."

The girls quickly rushed to Koko's car as the cop returned to her own vehicle. Koko started the engine and pulled away from the dance arena.

That night, Rhonda shared some of her thoughts on Facebook. "*Said goodbye to Claudia today. I'll miss her forever. But the funeral was the pits. Reminded me of my father's funeral a little. My grandmother forced me to go. He deserved to die for what he did to my mother all those years. Physical abuse, mental abuse. Too bad mom had to go to prison for it. She didn't deserve that. I don't deserve having to stay with my alcoholic grandmother either. That old lady is a real piece of work. I tried to escape for good before, but it didn't work. My therapist said I needed to work on standing my ground and facing my fears, but escaping this place is still on my mind. How did that preacher know?*"

A Flock of Crows

Rhonda hitchhiked from her grandmother's house to the Boarding School Road turnoff the first thing Memorial Day morning. On the rez, somebody would always pick you up when you needed a ride. No Uber needed.

After getting out of the rusted car and thanking the driver who gave her a lift, Rhonda hiked the short distance to the road that led to her uncle's house. While walking down the dirt road that led from the gate to Floyd's place, a faded memory suddenly popped into her mind. Once, a few years ago, when she was riding with her uncle on the same dirt road, he stopped the truck and got out.

"What are we stopping here for?" she asked him.

The land in that area was fairly flat, covered with very short grass strewn with small stones randomly scattered about.

"I want to show you something left here by your ancestors," he said as he walked a few yards away from the truck.

She caught up to him and followed as he headed toward a small rise in the ground.

When he stopped, he said, "Look down at the ground around here and tell me what you see."

Puzzled, she scanned the earth but didn't see anything unusual.

"If you look really close, you can just make out faint circles on the ground, some lined with small stones," he explained.

With added concentration, she tried again, and this time she saw the faint circular patterns. Each circle seemed to be about thirty feet across.

"I see them!" she exclaimed as she walked from one circle to another. "They're kind of like the circles in the grass at the powwow grounds."

Following the patterns, she discovered these circles were arranged to make one larger circle.

"The smaller circles are laid out in a big circle," she said excitedly. "But I never noticed them before. What are they? What made this pattern?"

"Tipis, just like at the powwow area," Floyd replied. "This is one of the places our ancestors regularly set up their camps long ago. Though this little rise is not very tall, you can see a long way across the prairie in every direction."

Rhonda clearly remembered that day all those years ago when she and her uncle stood on that spot for quite a while, soaking up the sun and listening to the gentle breeze.

"Close your eyes and imagine yourself two hundred years in the past," Floyd then said softly. "Feel the sun on your face and the earth beneath your feet. The sounds of our people freely living their traditional lives are all around you. You are at the center of the Blackfeet universe, and all is right with the world."

On that day Rhonda had smiled an enormous smile and felt an enormous satisfaction at just being herself.

Today, however, she felt nothing like that, and she could barely remember what it felt like to just be herself, to just be in a satisfying moment.

Dismissing the memory, Rhonda hurried along to her uncle's mobile home. Next to the manufactured dwelling stood an old log cabin with a caved-in roof. Floyd had always talked about "fixing her up and moving in," but he never did.

"Uncle Floyd," she called after opening the trailer's front door. "Are you here?"

"In the back, honey," he answered. "Be out in a minute."

While waiting, she helped herself to a cup of coffee from the freshly brewed pot on the kitchen counter.

"Ready to go?" Floyd asked as he entered the kitchen.

"What are we doing today?" Rhonda asked after taking a sip.

"You mean besides your graduation?" he quipped.

"I'm not going," Rhonda announced.

"Sure you are," her uncle proclaimed, opening a cardboard box that sat on the kitchen counter. He pulled out a black cap-and-gown outfit and held it up for her to see. The edges of the cap's square top had been beautifully beaded, and an eagle feather hung on a leather strap next to the tassel.

Rhonda didn't know what to say.

"Why don't you try it on?" Floyd asked.

He pulled the poncho-like black garment over his niece's head and let it drape down all around her. Then he placed the cap on her head, admired the outfit for a moment, and took a picture with his cell phone.

"Why don't you go to the hall mirror and take a look," he suggested.

When she saw herself, a small tear formed in the corner of one eye.

"I don't deserve this," she said and began removing the garment.

"No one deserves it *more*," her uncle said. "We have to celebrate the good moments of our lives to help us remember them during the bad times."

Rather than protest any further, Rhonda released her contrary thoughts and relaxed into the moment, just as her therapist had suggested. That made her feel a little better.

"Okay, I'll go to the graduation," she said. "But I don't really feel like celebrating."

"I know you don't," Floyd replied. "But you can honor yourself and your friend Claudia by finishing this one thing successfully. And finishing it means following through all the way until you have that diploma in your hand. That's something to be proud of, now and forever."

"Whatever," Rhonda said impatiently. "Now you're starting to sound like my therapist, and I don't need another one of those."

"I get it," her uncle said looking at his watch. "Now let's get to the high school before you miss the whole thing."

The pounding sound of powwow drums greeted Rhonda and Floyd as they approached the Browning High School gym. Parents, family members, and students flooded into the building for the ceremony. Floyd found a seat in the bleachers, and his niece took her assigned seat among the other graduates, who were excitedly chatting and goofing around before the ceremony began.

Rhonda noticed that several other graduating students wore caps that had been beaded in patterns similar to the one Floyd had given her. But to her, the graduates in their black robes looked like a flock of black birds hopping around on the ground, looking for crumbs of food.

Soon the drumming ended, and the school principal stepped up to the podium. Almost as soon as he started speaking, Rhonda began tuning out the man's voice. She was itching to pick up her phone and jump online to keep from being bored. But all devices were banned during the event. So instead, she closed her eyes and traveled in her mind.

At first, she was able to conjure up a fantasy scene where she was floating above the reservation. The buildings, streets, and cars looked so small below her. People seemed like ants. She felt safe there. For a while.

Then, from the west, the disturbing sound of squawking reached her ears. Looking in that direction, she saw a flying, swirling mass of dark objects moving toward her. As they came closer, she was able to see the mass was made up of angry crows. Before she could do anything, the crows surrounded her, beating her with their wings and pecking her with their sharp beaks.

She cried out in fear, but as soon as the sound left her mouth, she woke from the dark vision. That's when she realized everyone in the gym had heard her cry. It wasn't just in her mind. Everything in the gym had stopped. All eyes were on her.

Embarrassed, Rhonda jumped up from her seat and ran from the building. Seeing his niece in distress, Floyd quickly followed her outside. He found her sitting on a bench sobbing, with her head in her hands.

"Mind if I join you?" he asked as he stood beside her.

Rhonda just shrugged her shoulders and kept on sobbing.

He put a comforting hand on her shoulder and patted her a couple of times.

"Can we leave?" she managed to ask between sobs. "I can't handle going back in there."

"Can you handle a cheeseburger and fries?"

She nodded as her sobbing subsided, and the pair headed for Floyd's truck.

Over a satisfying meal of greasy comfort food at the Nation's Burger Station, Rhonda described the frightful vision she had in the gym.

"Somehow my mind still changes a perfectly normal event into something dark and threatening," she said after finishing the story. "At least, with the medication the doctor gave me, that's not happening as often."

"Your therapist said it will take some time," Floyd reminded her before popping a french fry into his mouth. After a pause, he added, "I'm sure we can get your diploma from the school in a couple of days. It'll be good to frame it and hang it on your bedroom wall."

"Whatever," the teenager replied with her favorite word. "It's not that big a deal."

Floyd decided *not* to explain once again exactly why it was a big deal. He let his niece finish her meal in peace.

A New Plan Is Hatched

"What can we do now?" Rhonda asked as she crumpled up the grease-soaked paper that had been wrapped around her burger. "Doing something physical helps me clear my mind."

"Old Mrs. White Swan does need some work done around her place," Floyd replied. "Her fence is down and her granddaughter's horse keeps trampling her garden. I think—"

"Let's go," Rhonda said before he could finish. She threw her trash in the nearest can and headed for her uncle's truck. Floyd gulped down his last bite of burger and ran to catch up to her.

Mrs. White Swan lived out west of town on Star School Road. They arrived in front of her place about fifteen minutes later. It was obvious that the frame house, barbed wire fence, and grounds could use some work. An Appaloosa horse, with its spotted coat, munched on tall weeds in the front yard.

"What first?" Rhonda asked, looking at all the work that needed to be done.

"Did you forget?" Floyd replied with a question of his own. "First, we go and respectfully greet her, show our respect, and ask her what she'd like us to do. Traditional way."

"Yeah, okay," the girl said, taking a few deep breaths. "Slow down and be here."

After greeting the elder and chatting a few moments, the pair finally began working. Floyd led the horse into the small pasture behind the house and began repairing the fence. Rhonda set about repairing the woman's front steps, which were in danger of collapsing. She continued with similar repairs to the outside of the house, using skills she'd learned from her uncle.

The afternoon zipped by, and before long, the sun again began to set beyond the mountains in the west called the Backbone of the World. Mrs. White Swan brought out two paper plates filled with Indian tacos piled high with meat, beans, and cheese. Bottled water rounded out the meal, which Rhonda scarfed down in no time.

All in all, Rhonda had a good day after surviving the imagined attack of crows.

After giving her a twenty-dollar bill for the afternoon's work, Floyd delivered his niece to the front of her grandmother's house. Before she got out of the truck, he reminded her that it wouldn't be too long before she could move out of that house.

"In the meantime, you can practice patience," he added as she got out.

Thankfully the house was empty, and Rhonda knew her grandmother was probably at her favorite place, the tribe's casino. After a quick shower, the girl lay on the bed in her favorite pajamas, which were cut-off shorts and a T-shirt. She turned on her aging computer. It was time to see what social media chatter had been generated by her freak-out session during graduation earlier in the day.

There were the usual mean-spirited comments from other Native teens, calling her things like "psycho-girl" and saying she was "too chicken to go through with it," referring to her suicide attempt. Moving on, Rhonda navigated to see what had shown up in her news feed. She watched a graduation video posted by a parent until it came to the moment when she'd fled the gymnasium.

Thinking of Claudia, Rhonda typed a couple of words and made a couple of clicks, which took her to Claudia's Facebook page. Still active. No one had closed the account. Scrolling down the timeline, she came across photos of a few past events that brought back fond memories.

But she could feel the familiar dark, depressive emotions coming on as she thought about her dead friend. It was time to move on.

Then, when she scrolled over a picture of a Native girl standing in front of a group of tents, a video started playing.

"I'm standing in front of our encampment on the Standing Stone Indian Reservation," the girl, who looked to be about Rhonda's age, said. "In case you haven't heard, we've come to protest the pipeline a big oil company wants to build across sacred tribal homeland. They've already started plowing up the soil, and their path will put the pipeline directly under the river that is the main source of water for wildlife and Natives in this area."

The camera zoomed out to reveal more of the encampment. Rhonda could see dozens of tents of all sizes mixed in with several tipis sitting clustered beside the river.

"People from the nearby reservations and communities have been coming to help with the protest over the past few weeks," the girl continued. "Our camp is growing, and we're running low on basic necessities."

The camera panned to the right and stopped on a group of wooden pallets sitting on the ground.

One was stacked with plastic bottles of water. Another held cans of food. A third pallet supported large cardboard boxes with the word "clothing" written on the side.

"We desperately need food, water, clothing—whatever you can spare," the girl said. "My name is Pamela Chesalo, from the Wind River Reservation, and I'm just one of several youth from our rez camped out here."

The camera panned back over to Pamela, who was now surrounded by a group of Native teens. They held a large banner emblazoned with the words "Water is Life!"

The whole story fascinated Rhonda. She watched the video a second time, paying more attention to what was going on in the background. Something clicked in her mind, and she made a decision. She was going to collect donations from people on her rez and take them to the Standing Stone encampment.

"*Just hatched a new plan,*" Rhonda immediately texted to her buddies, Nadie and Koko. "*Can you swing by to pick me up in 15 minutes to discuss?*"

Within minutes, she heard from both of them. Two thumbs up!

Careful not to wake her grandmother, who had returned home, Rhonda slipped out of the house and waited at the curb. When her friends rolled up, she jumped in the back seat. On the way to the Towne Pump for a late-night snack, Rhonda laid out her idea.

"Wait, what?" Nadie said after hearing the plan. "You want us to collect donations from people on this rez, and then drive seven hundred miles to deliver them to a bunch of people camped out on another rez?"

"Well, there's a lot more to it than that," Rhonda replied with exasperation. "Those people are there to protect their land and water, to support an important cause!"

That's when Rhonda remembered the words of the preacher. He'd said, "Your best means of escape is to take on a cause bigger than yourself, somewhere beyond this place, where you can channel your energy to protect someone or something that needs your help."

Then, out loud, she said to her friends, "I think this may be the cause I'm supposed to take on. You know, the message from Claudia's funeral."

They sat in silence thinking about things for a moment.

"We need to support Rhonda on this," Koko said to Nadie with a sense of finality. "Whether we think it's crazy or not, we should help her do this."

"Okay," Nadie said with reluctance. Then she added with a smile, "I guess we can help out psycho-girl here."

After a quiet few seconds, all three girls broke out in laughter.

The next morning, Rhonda phoned her uncle.

"Did you ever get that old Ford truck of yours running?" she asked him. "The one with the carburetor I tried to fix."

"Sure did," Floyd said. "It needed a new starter motor. It looks a little rough, but it works."

"Can I borrow it?" she asked.

"What for?"

"To collect donations from people around here and then drive them to the Standing Stone Reservation," she said, and then explained the whole situation to him.

"Are you planning to do all that by yourself?" Floyd said.

"Nadie and Koko said they'd help get donations and take them to the protest site with me," she assured him.

"I tell you what," her uncle said after some thought. "What if I drive you around to all the people I've done work for in the past? They certainly should be open to making some kind of donation. They owe me."

And so for the next few days that's just what they did. Koko and Nadie used Koko's car to visit all their relatives and extended family members as well. The Blackfeet people surprised Rhonda with their generous contributions. Within four days, they'd collected enough clothing, blankets, canned goods, bottled water, and other stuff to fill the pickup bed to overflowing.

Word spread across the rez about the project, and some cash donations came in as well. There was enough to pay for gas and food for the drive to the other rez in North Dakota and back again. The response was so encouraging, Rhonda started to feel that this might be one of the few things in her life she didn't fail at.

Floyd had an old camper shell lying around, which he installed in the back over the truck's bed. This would prevent any of the donated items from blowing away during the trip. The next morning, he filled the truck's gas tank using some of the donated cash.

Meanwhile, Rhonda had gotten up early and left a note for her grandmother, the "warden," about the trip. Koko and Nadie picked her up and off they went to Floyd's house.

Using Rhonda's phone, Floyd took a picture of the three girl adventurers in front of the dented, rusting, brown-and-beige 1978 Ford pickup. Then he hugged his niece, telling her, "This will be good for you. I think this is the best decision you've made in a long time, so take your time and don't rush back."

With that, the threesome jumped in the truck's cab and headed off down the road. The plan was to take turns driving the twelve or more hours so they'd arrive at the pipeline protest encampment by the end of the day.

To save time, all their meals came from fast food restaurants with drive-through service. And any time there was a cell phone signal along the way, whoever wasn't driving posted messages and selfies on Twitter, Instagram, and Facebook to announce their trip to deliver the donations.

This was really the first time Rhonda had been excited about anything in a long while, and her social media posts reflected it.

"*Can't wait to get to the Standing Stone pipeline protest camp*," one of her tweets read. "*Water is life! Everybody knows that! We have to protect it!*"

As the sun set and darkness descended on them, the girls discovered that the old truck's headlights were too dim to drive at night. Luckily, a billboard directed them to the Butte View public campground outside of Bodine, North Dakota.

As they pulled into the campground, Nadie, who was never the best at spelling, asked, "Why would anyone name a place Butt View?"

Rhonda and Koko just looked at each other.

"And just whose butt would we have to view?" she continued.

Koko explained the difference between butte and butt to Nadie while Rhonda used some of their donated cash to pay for a camping spot for the night. The girls crashed quickly in the back of the truck, lying in their bedrolls on a layer of donated clothes.

Unspoken Words

Sleepy-eyed, the girls awoke shortly after sunrise, which was very unusual for them when there was no school. According to the Butte View Campground manager, their destination, the northern entrance to the Standing Stone Reservation, was only about an hour and a half away.

After throwing out all the food wrappers from the previous day and eating a quick breakfast purchased from the campground's store/café, the travelers pushed on. Rhonda's excitement grew as the miles flew by. Within an hour or so, she made the final turn that put them on the road that led to the encampment. Driving southward on the two-lane blacktop, the three travelers came to the crest of a hill where Rhonda suddenly hit the brakes.

"Why are we stopping?" Nadie asked as Rhonda killed the engine and jumped out of the truck's cab.

Rhonda pointed with her lips to the river valley below them, then answered, "That's why."

Laid out before them was a scene none of the girls had ever witnessed before. To the left was a wide, lazy river flowing gently southward. Straight ahead of them, down the road in the distance, was a sign that announced, "NOW ENTERING STANDING STONE INDIAN RESERVATION." Nearer to them, on the banks of the river, was an encampment made up of a few haphazardly arranged tents and tipis interspersed with cars and trucks. The camp was dotted with a few colorful flags. Dozens of people, both Native and non-Native, seemed to be busy with day-to-day camping life.

To Rhonda's right, much farther inland, was an entirely separate group of people. There were men in brown work clothes, surrounded by large pieces of equipment, including graders, dozers, and dump trucks. The large vehicles were parked in a line. Just behind these men and their machinery were stacks and stacks of large metal pipes: the makings of a pipeline. And behind that, stretching to the northwest beyond the horizon, was a long swath of land that had been plowed and cleared of prairie grasses. The long strip of bare soil looked like a black snake slithering toward them. It was obvious that the snake would eventually reach the river.

In between the blacktop road and the machinery, a backcountry gravel road stretched westward. Spread out along the gravel road, a small line of protestors holding signs and banners marched toward the construction workers and their machines.

"Water is life!" the protestors chanted in unison as they marched. "You're trampling sacred ground!"

The pipeline workers shook their fists at the protestors, and one of them with a megaphone shouted, "You're anti-American!" and "You're nothing but a bunch of terrorists!"

Rhonda pulled out her cell phone, took a couple of pictures, and then posted them online with the message, "*We made it all the way to the pipeline protest at Standing Stone. This is something to see. Pipeline workers and machinery to the right, the river and camp to the left, and a line of protesters in the middle.*"

When she finished posting, she told her friends, "We got to get down there," and jumped back in the truck.

"Wait!" Nadie yelled back at her. "You want to get into the middle of that?"

"That's what we came for, isn't it?" Rhonda replied, nodding her head.

"But, I'm confused," Nadie said. "When it comes to conflict, you usually run for cover."

"I know," Rhonda said, "But my uncle and my therapist keep saying I need to learn to face my fears and try new ways of dealing with stuff."

Nadie and Koko just looked at each other.

"Come on! Get in! Let's just go!" Rhonda said impatiently. "If I put this off, I might chicken out."

Realizing this is what their friend needed, Nadie and Koko got into the truck, and Rhonda headed down the hill. She made a beeline for the heart of the camp and spotted an area stacked with pallets of goods: bottled water, cans of food, and boxes of clothing. Nearby sat a large tent that was actually constructed out of several smaller tents stitched together. A large, hand-lettered cardboard sign on one side announced, "KITCHEN."

Rhonda parked the truck close to the pallets, got out, and began looking for someone who might be in charge of things. Nadie and Koko got out and started looking around the camp. A familiar-looking girl stepped out of the kitchen tent.

"We've brought donations from Blackfeet," Rhonda told her. "Should we unload them here or somewhere else?"

Rhonda recognized her as the girl in the Facebook video.

"You're Pamela, aren't you?" Rhonda asked. "The one online asking for donations?"

"Yeah, that's me," Pamela answered. "Call me Pam. I'm sort of the supply clerk for the camp. Let's see what you've got."

Rhonda opened up the back of the camper shell and dropped the tailgate so Pam could see the load they had carried from Browning.

"Impressive," Pam said. "I'll call some guys to come and get it unloaded."

"We can handle it," Rhonda replied, and she called for Nadie and Koko to come help. When the four girls finished with the task, Pam invited them to stick around.

"We'll be serving a meal in a little while," she explained. "After that, if you're interested, we'll get an update from the Standing Stone Tribal Council on the status of the tribe's attempt to legally stop construction of the pipeline."

"Absolutely," Rhonda replied with excitement. "What's going on over there where the protestors are lined up?"

"That's just the daily standoff," Pam said. "Pipeline construction has halted for the time being, thanks to temporary legal action against the energy company. This afternoon's meeting should tell us if the injunction will hold or if the judge will allow construction to continue."

"How long have you been camped out here?" Rhonda asked.

"Since April, after a Standing Stone tribal elder heard about the pipeline plan and set up her camp here by the river," Pam answered. "This is her land, and she was the first one out here."

Pam excused herself saying she needed to take care of a logistical emergency.

"So, what's the plan?" Nadie asked Rhonda. "We delivered the goods. Ready to head home now?"

"I'd like to hang around awhile just to see what's what," Rhonda replied. "It wouldn't hurt to stay a day."

"Sounds sketchy," Koko said. "But not much is happening back home, so why not!"

The girls headed for the line of protesters to see what that was about. Up the gravel road, about forty people of all ages stood in a line facing the dormant tractors and trucks. No one in the line spoke. They just stood there quietly facing the pipeline workers and their equipment. Many held signs saying, "NO PIPELINE," and "YOU'RE ON SACRED GROUND," and "OIL AND WATER DON'T MIX."

"No one's doing anything," Nadie complained. "What kind of protest is this?"

Rhonda shushed her friend and studied the situation for a moment. It seemed quiet and nonthreatening, so she found an empty space between two protesters and stepped into line. She signaled Nadie and Koko, encouraging them to join her, but the two weren't into it at all. Silently, the pair shook their heads and turned away, heading back toward the camp.

But the line of focused, silent protesters somehow spoke to Rhonda. A subtle yet powerful energy began to flow through her as soon as she made herself a part of the line. An understanding came into her mind, an understanding of what was at stake here in this seemingly ordinary, out-of-the-way place.

No words were spoken, but Rhonda heard a voice in her head. Was the voice coming from the minds of these people? Or was it coming from somewhere deeper? Wherever it originated, it communicated something meaningful to her.

This is sacred ancient land. Our ancestors lived and died on this soil. The water in this river is sacred water that feeds all living things nearby. Constructing a pipeline to carry oil through here defiles this land. If the pipeline spills its contents, it will contaminate this water. It has no place here. Our lives and our bodies are a testament to these truths. Enough is enough. We stand together as the last line of defense for the spirit of the earth and the water.

Rhonda couldn't begin to understand how she "heard" those unspoken words. She had never felt anything like what she was feeling at the moment, and she didn't want it to stop. But she had a decision to make. Should she follow the path of least resistance like she usually did, or should she let go of her fears and move in an entirely new direction?

In the past, trying to make a decision like this one would have paralyzed Rhonda. But in the midst of weighing those questions, the words of her therapist came into the girl's head. "*Our daily lives are made up of countless small and large decisions, but sometimes it's hard to tell them apart. Make every decision with care, because you never know which one could change your life in ways you never dreamed of.*"

At that moment, Rhonda made up her mind. Actually, somewhere at a deep level in her brain, the decision was made for her. With a sense of finality, she realized this was her place, and this was the cause she was meant to take up.

The Elder Speaks

For lunch, Pam and the volunteer kitchen staff served up heaping bowls of corn soup to everyone in the camp. Calling it corn soup, however, really didn't do justice to the mix of corn, carrots, potatoes, beans, meat, and spices. Rhonda thought it was the best meal she'd had in a long time. Nadie and Koko, on the other hand, just thought it was a bowl of soup.

"I can tell this isn't your thing, so you two should just go on home," she told them. "Me, I'm staying. It feels like this is where I need to be."

Rhonda's friends couldn't believe what they were hearing.

"You know, in a couple of days you'll be calling up and begging us to come get you," Koko said.

Ignoring her comment, Rhonda said, "Take the truck back to my uncle's house and tell him I'll be just fine here."

"This is really the first time you've ever left Blackfeet," Nadie reminded Rhonda. "Why here? Why now?"

"I can't explain it," Rhonda replied. "But I know there's nothing for me back home. You two are headed off to college in the fall, and I'm not college material."

Nadie and Koko remained silent, not convinced this was the best choice for their friend.

"I'll be fine," Rhonda said, sensing what her friends were thinking. "This really is the best thing for me."

She reached in her pocket and pulled out the truck keys and the leftover traveling cash. Rhonda counted out enough money for gas and food for the girls' return trip, handed the bills to Koko, and put the rest back in her own pocket.

Pam walked over and joined them, so Rhonda asked, "Got any place a girl can crash for the night?"

"The big lodge over there is the women's sleeping quarters," Pam replied. "You're welcome to stay there. The boys' tipi is down by the river."

Turning back to her friends, Rhonda said, "See? I'll be fine."

Realizing that her friend had made up her mind, Koko stuffed the money in her pocket and gave Rhonda a hug.

"You be safe," she said. "Keep us posted on what's going on, okay?"

"I will," Rhonda agreed as she gave Nadie a hug too.

Nadie and Koko headed for the truck, and Rhonda turned her attention back to Pam and the camp.

"I'm here to help," the teen said. "What can I do?"

"What *can* you do?" Pamela returned the question.

"Fix things, I guess," the Blackfeet girl replied with a shrug of her shoulders. "Repair old cars, fences, and houses. Stuff I learned from my uncle. Oh, and herd cattle, feed horses, and chop firewood. You know—rez stuff."

Pam smiled broadly and was about to speak when she saw two people coming toward her.

"Later I'll get you over to the camp's maintenance guy, Billy Old Bull," Pam said as she began walking away. "But our guests have arrived, and everyone in camp will want to hear what they have to say."

Pam walked briskly toward the guests. One of them was a Native man wearing boots, jeans, and a cowboy hat, who appeared to be in his forties.

The other was an elderly Native woman wearing a flowered blouse, full-length dress, and dance shawl around her shoulders.

As Pam escorted the two guests into the camp's central lodge, a young Native man wearing a blue jean jacket with a large AIM patch on the back stepped out of the kitchen tent. He faced north, placed a powered megaphone to his lips, and made an announcement.

"Tribal chairman Solomon Smoke and elder Maxine Little Moon have arrived," he said. "Come to the main lodge for an update on the court decision."

He rotated to the other three directions and repeated the announcement to make sure everyone in the camp heard him.

About a hundred people quietly crowded into the large tipi that stood in the center of the camp. Rhonda didn't know exactly what the meeting was about, but she could tell it was important. Tension hung in the air as the campers got settled on the ground or stood in the back of the circular space. The tribal chairman and the elder stood in the front near an easel that held a large map.

"I'm sorry to say I have bad news for you today," Chairman Smoke began.

Rhonda could feel the energy level inside the lodge immediately drop as a collective sigh escaped the lips of everyone present.

"For those of you new to our camp, let me catch you up to where we are," he said and pointed to a red diagonal line that cut across the map.

"If completed, this pipeline will stretch some twelve hundred miles, from the oil fields of North Dakota to refineries in Illinois," the chairman continued. "They've completed about half that distance, which brought them to our location here."

He tapped his forefinger on a green area in the middle of the map.

"Something called an easement, like a permit, is needed for every piece of land where the pipeline is to be laid, but no easement has been granted for this strip of land just outside the reservation."

He flipped the top map over to reveal a second map that showed a close-up of the green area on the map.

"This green area is part of ancient land belonging to the Great Sioux Nation, and though it's not part of the Standing Stone Reservation, it is part of land promised to us in treaties. So the tribe filed a motion, called an injunction, in court to stop them from building on this land."

Chairman Smoke stepped away from the map and faced the gathered group.

"I'm sorry to say that yesterday the judge ruled against our injunction," he said. "Construction of the pipeline is set to resume within a week."

Disappointment spread across the crowd as people began discussing this news in hushed tones. Rhonda thought that maybe it meant the protest was over, that everyone would pack up and leave. She'd just arrived and felt good about being part of this movement. Now it would end? Would this be another failure to add to her list?

"Quiet, please," the young man said through his megaphone. "Our elder has something to say."

The crowd grew silent as the young man held the megaphone for the elder to speak into it. She shook her head, signaling that she didn't need to use it. Surprised, the young man stepped away.

"It is true that we are few in number and seemingly powerless, while the oil company and their friends in the government are many in number and all-powerful," the elder woman said in a voice much louder than seemed possible. "But Native peoples have faced these odds before, and I believe Tunkashila, Grandfather Creator, is with us. Or should I say, we are with him."

She paused, waiting until a few stragglers entered the lodge and got settled in the back.

"Ancient tribal prophecy warned of the coming of a terrible Black Snake that will desecrate our land and spoil our water," she continued. "I tell you this pipeline is that Black Snake!"

A gasp spread through the room amid whispered chatter that began to grow louder.

"Please quiet down so our elder can speak," came the voice of the young man through the megaphone.

The lodge immediately fell silent again.

"Water is life, and this land is sacred to us. The land and the water need protection from this Black Snake, and I for one am here to be a protector. And if you choose to remain here with me to fight, you too are protectors. No longer are we pipeline protestors. We are Water Protectors!"

Every single person in that lodged jumped to their feet as a roar of approval and excitement rang out. A powerful sense of energy flowed through them.

The tribal chairman took the megaphone and spoke to the noisy crowd.

"You protesters, I mean protectors, have been effective in slowing down the construction while the tribe and others attempt to stop the pipeline in the courts," he said. "Our next move will be to legally force the oil company to do a study of the pipeline's environmental impact on the river. So we ask you to keep up the fight!"

As Chairman Smoke set the megaphone down, the closest people in the audience stepped forward and formed a line. One by one, they shook the elder's hand and the hand of the tribal chairman. As they did so, they made a vow to stay and fight.

Before the chairman left, he spoke to Pam.

"When this bad news came in, the members of the Standing Stone Tribal Council voted to more fully support this protest camp and request the support of the other tribes in this region," he said. "Just let us know what you need, and we'll try to get it out here as quick as possible."

Pam, who stood near Rhonda, leaned over to her and asked, "Are you in? Are you staying?"

"Are you kidding?" Rhonda replied. "I'm in all the way!"

"Good. You got a phone and a Facebook account?"

"Of course, but I need to charge the phone," Rhonda explained. "It's dead. How am I going to charge it?"

"With the generator the tribe loaned us," Pam replied, pointing to a truck parked at the edge of the camp. "And that includes a Wi-Fi hot spot. The password is 'sacredground,' all lowercase, no spaces."

"Impressive!" Rhonda said, echoing Pam's earlier response to the Browning teen's donation.

"While your phone is charging, pass the word to everyone in the camp to put out the call to anyone and everyone we know to come and help,"

Pam said. "Start with Facebook friends and other social media contacts. Later, we'll work on new strategies for protest."

As Rhonda headed for the generator truck, Pam called out, "The youth in the camp are meeting at sundown in the boys' tipi by the river. I expect to see you there!"

Rhonda gave her the thumbs-up sign and dug her charging cable out of her back pocket. After plugging in her phone and entering the password, she typed her first post. *"Calling all protectors of earth and water! An elder called the oil pipeline being built here the Black Snake, and that's exactly what I saw when I arrived today. The Black Snake represents pollution and desecration of sacred land and water. We must stop it dead in its tracks! Please come and help us!"*

Shedding the Old Skin

As the sun began to set, the tipis and tents of the encampment began to glow from the inside as campers lit kerosene lamps and battery-powered lanterns. Rhonda had managed to find a vacant spot inside the women's lodge to spread out the sleeping bag she'd brought for the trip. After saying hello to the two older Native women who would be sleeping closest to her in the tipi, she set off for the youth meeting.

A small fire burned in the center of the men's tipi, the site of the youth meeting. A wisp of gray smoke from the fire lazily drifted upward and through the smoke hole at the top of the lodge. About a dozen Native young people, including Pam, were sitting around the fire, either on the ground or on wood crates. Three other young

Natives, two girls and a boy, stood in an open space in the circle. Rhonda found a vacant crate and took a seat, not knowing what to expect from the gathering.

"The words from our elder Maxine Little Moon today have inspired and challenged us as Native youth," Pam said. "We already know we need to take action quickly to stop the pipeline. The question is, what action will we take? I've asked Mona, Wanda, and Michael from the nearby Arapaho River Rez to share some of their past experiences with previous environmental action."

The dark-skinned girl with short black hair and a small ring in her nose spoke first.

"I'm Mona, from Arapaho River, not far from here," she said. "This is not the first proposed oil pipeline that could contaminate tribal waters. Over the last few years, our tribe has been using the legal system to try and stop the proposed Greystone XL pipeline that could eventually be built near our lands."

Then Mona moved closer to the seated circle of youth.

"But things aren't so great on our rez," she said in a quiet voice. "You may have heard about the youth suicides there."

Rhonda's ears immediately perked up.

"A very wise elder back home said that young people needed a mission," Mona continued. "Something that would keep us focused on a goal and busy working to reach that goal. So we formed a youth council on our rez to deal with these issues and to help young people like us cope and lift our spirits."

The second girl, who was lighter-skinned with long braided hair, spoke next.

"After getting educated about the possible Greystone construction, we decided to put up what we called a Spirit Camp, so we'd have a place just for youth to go and pray, sing, and hold ceremonies. That really helped us become a group who cared about each other, and at the same time gave us a way to contribute to the protection of our lands."

Michael, displaying an eagle tattoo on his left arm, stepped forward and spoke.

"So we think that's what you guys should do here," he said. "Establish a youth Spirit Camp for prayer and ceremony, and then invite Native youth from other reservations to join in. We can help you get started if you want."

Surprising herself, Rhonda excitedly shot up her hand as if she was in a classroom and said, "I nominate Pam to be chairman of our group or club or whatever it is!"

This took everyone by surprise, and for a moment, no one said or did anything.

"I second that!" a girl sitting on the opposite side of the circle suddenly exclaimed. "I think that's what you're supposed to do."

"I third it!" the boy sitting next to her said. "Are there thirds?"

Laughter broke out around the circle as Pam stood up.

"Hold on," Pam said. "Not so fast. Don't we need to vote on the idea of creating this youth council?"

Everyone in the circle immediately raised their hands.

"I guess that settles that," Pam said.

Then they all started talking at once, spouting ideas about what needed doing next. Pam broke through the chaos to bring some order back to the meeting and began creating a to-do list for them.

So many tasks needed doing, and everything was a priority. Among other things, they needed to see if anyone in the camp or on the Standing Stone Tribal Council had a tipi the youth could borrow for the Spirit Camp. And although each of them chose tasks to carry out in the days to come, all their activities needed to be coordinated with the camp's adult leaders, of course.

It was too dark to go in search of a tipi for the Spirit Camp lodge, so that would wait until tomorrow. In the meantime, the teens talked about a name for themselves. Someone suggested National Native Youth Council, but after discussion, it was decided that they wanted to be able to include Canadian Native youth as well. The word "international" needed to be in there somewhere. They finally and unanimously settled on International Council of Native Youth, or ICNY for short.

After her surprising and spontaneous nomination of Pam, Rhonda mostly watched the rest of the group's interaction from the fringe of the circle, her usual mode when faced with groups of people she didn't know. Everyone was friendly enough, but she still had some trouble letting down her guard or allowing strangers to get very close.

Pam, who had no trouble making new friends or taking charge, noticed Rhonda's reluctance to fully participate. Quietly, she settled in beside the Blackfeet teen and started a conversation.

"Your input is as valid as anyone's," Pam told Rhonda. "I mean, you might have ideas or experiences that no one else has that could be keys to solving problems that need solving."

"I'm not comfortable talking in a group, especially with people I don't know," Rhonda responded. "I'm more of a doer."

"All right, I get it," Pam replied. "Tomorrow you'll get your chance to be a doer, and thanks for stepping up to volunteer. This camp will be a better place with you in it."

That night, as she slept on the ground in her sleeping bag in the women's lodge, Rhonda had a dream. She was walking in a deep, dark canyon with steep walls on either side of her. The girl felt lost, not able to find a way out of the canyon. Then something shiny on the ground caught her eye. Looking more closely, she saw that it was a razor blade. In the dream she said, "Aha! That's what I've been looking for."

The dream version of Rhonda picked up the blade and began cutting her wrists, first the left one and then the right. But no blood came from the shallow cuts. Instead, her outer layer of skin became loose. She began peeling away the extra skin, and all over her body this outer layer fell away. Like a snake shedding a layer of dead skin, Rhonda shed this old skin. Underneath there was a whole new layer of fresh skin. It was as if she was being born again.

Dawn of a New Day

At first light the next morning, Rhonda awoke feeling fresh. Lying in her sleeping bag, she gazed up through the smoke hole of the tipi and saw clear blue sky above. Then she remembered last night's dream and abruptly sat up.

Quickly she checked her wrists to see if there were new any cuts, but she found only the scars left from her failed suicide attempt back in March. Relieved, she rubbed her forearms. Same old skin as before.

Then something her therapist said popped into her mind. "*Symbolically, death may not be the end of life, and if you dream of death, it probably means that the old you is dying so a new you can come to life. It's a chance to begin again.*"

That's when the teen realized no one in the camp knew the old Rhonda, so she was free to reinvent herself and become a new Rhonda. How did that corny old saying go? Today is the first day of the rest of your life? Well, this day surely was.

She made a quick visit to the kitchen tent for a fast breakfast and set out to see what this new life would bring. Pam said she needed to find Billy Old Bull, head of the camp's ground crew. So finding Billy was next on Rhonda's agenda. He was described as being as big as a buffalo, tough as an ox, and yet as tender as a teddy bear.

She found a large Native man fitting that description supporting a long pole near the camp's central tipi. With the help of two other Indian men who looked a lot alike, he was in the process of raising a flagpole that held the Standing Stone tribal flag.

"Could you grab that post-hole digger and clear a little more dirt out of that hole?" the big man asked Rhonda as she approached. "We got to get more depth to stabilize this thing."

Seeing the tool laying on the ground beside the hole, the teen said, "Sure."

Experienced with fence repairs back home, she picked up the post-hole digger and shoved the blades deep into the opening in the ground. With a few quick moves, she pulled several more inches of dirt out of the hole.

"Give that a try," she said as she took a few steps back.

The three men slid the bottom end of the pole into the enlarged hole and hoisted the long shaft upward as they marched along its length. Their steady movement raised it to a vertical position. The two look-alikes began shoveling in dirt around the bottom of the pole.

Billy dusted off his large, stubby hands and asked, "Are you Rhonda?"

"Yep," she replied as she shook his extended hand.

"Excuse the grease," he said apologetically.

"Not worried about a little grease," Rhonda said as she shook the man's dirty hand, which felt like a vice clamp.

"Good at working outdoors?" he asked.

"Fair," she answered. "Thanks to my uncle."

Billy pointed with his lips at his two helpers, then added, "These are two of my go-to crew guys, Bo and Bubba. They're brothers, if you couldn't tell."

Rhonda shook both their hands. The older one, Bubba, probably in his thirties, had short hair and a military insignia tattooed on his upper arm. Bo, who appeared to be in his twenties, sported long hair tied in a single braid and a red bandana.

"Welcome aboard the ground crew," he said with a smile. "We ain't pretty, but we get the job done, whatever job needs doing."

The strains of a powwow song bellowed from Billy's back pocket, and he reached around to extract his singing cell phone.

"If we don't know how to do something, we fake it till we make it," he told Rhonda before taking the call. After listening intently for a few seconds, he said to the caller, "Be there in a flash to get 'em."

He ended the call, turned back to his crew, and said, "Those walkie-talkie radios finally came in, guys. We can go pick them up."

Realizing that he now had a new addition to the crew who wasn't a guy, he corrected himself. "Oops. Sorry. Not used to having a girl—"

"Now don't start getting all soft on me," Rhonda said with a friendly grin. "You can think of me as just one of the guys."

That satisfied Billy, and off he marched, with the brothers and Rhonda not far behind.

They headed toward a large green army tent that stood near the north end of the camp. A plywood sign beside it read simply "HQ," for headquarters.

Inside the tent, tables, chairs, and various kinds of equipment had been set up, including portable TVs, radios, and laptop computers. Rhonda could hear the sound of a generator running outside the tent that provided electricity for the electrical gear.

On one table sat four rows of charging bases that held four walkie-talkies each. Billy pulled radios for himself and his three assistants out of their chargers and showed Rhonda how to use hers. Then he made sure they were all tuned to the same frequency.

"We've got to get to the south end of the encampment to lay out a grid," Billy told them while leading them toward a pickup truck. "They're expecting more campers to start arriving tonight and tomorrow."

And off they went.

As they tackled whatever job needed doing the rest of the day, they got used to each other's way of working. They quickly and easily gelled into a team. The tasks alternated between muscle work and brain work. Some tasks required a strong back, so Rhonda allowed the boys to handle those heavier loads. Other duties called for a quick mind to figure out how to get a job done, often without the proper tools or hardware at hand. That's where Rhonda seemed to shine, again thanks to skills learned from Uncle Floyd.

The day passed quickly, and before Rhonda realized it, the sun was casting long, late-afternoon shadows on the ground. Billy told his team to take a quick break.

As Rhonda took a long, slow drink of water from a tin cup that hung from the big, plastic water tank near the kitchen, she saw a caravan of cars, trucks, and vans moving down the road that ran along the west side of the camp.

"We ain't done yet," Billy's voice boomed from Rhonda's radio. "We've got to make sure the folks in that caravan pull into the new camping sites we set up. Come on!"

Rhonda took one final gulp and ran off to catch up. From that moment forward, it seemed like everything in the camp shifted into high gear.

That night Rhonda collapsed into her bedroll with satisfied exhaustion and had the most peaceful sleep of her seventeen years of life.

Early next morning, she awoke to the smell of coffee. Her eyes opened to find Pam standing at the foot of her bedroll holding two cups of the stuff.

"It's morning already?" Rhonda sleepily asked in disbelief. "Feels like I just closed my eyes a minute ago."

"Time for a sunrise ceremony," Pam said, thrusting a cup toward her. "The International Council of Native Youth are hosting it at our new Spirit Camp lodge."

That got Rhonda awake and excited.

"We have a Spirit Camp lodge?" she asked as she slipped on a shirt and pair of jeans. "When did that happen?"

"While you were off being one of the guys," Pam replied.

Rhonda took a sip of caffeine juice to see how hot it was and found that it was just right. She slurped half the cup in a couple of gulps before following Pam out of the lodge. They headed north along the river.

"So who loaned us the lodge and the ground to put it on?" Rhonda asked as they walked.

"It's a twofer," Pam said jokingly.

"A what?"

"A twofer," Pam repeated. "We got the lodge and the land from the same person. And on top of that, the lodge had already been put up."

"That's awesome," Rhonda said as she finished off her coffee. "So, who do we have to thank for all that?"

"Elder Maxine Little Moon," Pam said. "This encampment sits on property her family owns just outside the reservation boundary, and she put up the first protest lodge here. She offered it for our use."

"Cool," Rhonda said. "Totally cool."

"Oh, and everyone just calls her Grandma," Pam said. "She's everybody's grandmother around here."

"She sounds nothing like *my* grandmother," Rhonda said. "I'd like to meet her."

"You will, in just a few minutes," Pam said as the pair approached the Spirit Camp.

A large, beautifully painted tipi sat on a low hill overlooking the river and the rest of the camp. Parked beside the tipi was a tan-and-green RV that displayed the word "Winnebago" in gold letters on one side.

The door flap of the tipi faced eastward toward the rising sun. Pam and Rhonda entered. Inside the lodge, the young Natives of the International Council of Native Youth were gathered around Maxine Little Moon—Grandma. The elder was seated on a small wooden bench. Pam led Rhonda over to the gathering.

"Sorry we're late," she said as they entered the circle of people.

"Come here, child," Grandma said to Rhonda. The twinkle in her eyes accented her kind and wrinkled face. "Let me get a better look at you."

Slowly, reluctantly, Rhonda approached the elder.

"Give me your hand," the woman said in a quiet, comforting voice.

Rhonda reached out her left hand, palm down. With a smile, Grandma reached out her own hand, palm up, and took hold of Rhonda's with a gentle but firm grip. Then the elder placed her other hand on top of Rhonda's and looked into the girl's eyes.

"I'm so glad you decided to stay with us," Grandma said. "Pam told me how you brought donations from your reservation and felt like you belonged here."

Without breaking contact with Rhonda's eyes, Grandma turned the girl's hand over and gently rubbed the teen's forearm and wrist. There, of course, the elder felt the three-month-old scars left by the razor blade. Normally, Rhonda would have flinched or pulled her arm back, but she didn't.

The old woman's gaze penetrated the girl's defenses and seemed to strip her soul bare. But it wasn't a threatening gaze. It felt to Rhonda like she was being bathed in a warm pool of soothing energy.

"Many people, young and old, Native and non-Native, are coming here to save Mother Earth and fight against the pipeline," Grandma said in a quiet voice. "But they're really coming here to heal themselves, to save *themselves*. Just like you, young lady."

Rhonda's eyes began to water, as deep emotion welled up inside her. How did this woman know?

"If you wouldn't mind keeping an old lady company," Grandma said, still looking into Rhonda's eyes, "I'd like to invite you stay with me while you're here at the camp."

A whispered gasp spread through the circle of youth, any one of whom would have given up their smartphone for such an invitation.

"I . . . I don't know what to say," Rhonda replied.

"Just say yes, dear," Grandma said. "That's all you have to say."

"Yes," Rhonda answered. "Of course, yes."

Grandma patted Rhonda's hand and turned to the rest of the group.

"Every one of you is invited to bring your tents or tipis or minivans—whatever you're staying in—up here to the Spirit Camp," she said. "This place is yours to use, and I expect great things from you."

That brought big grins to all their faces.

"Now, let's get that sunrise ceremony done," she said.

After the ceremony, Rhonda returned to the women's lodge to retrieve her sleeping bag and other belongings. Then she scurried back to the Spirit Camp lodge to deposit them. Just as she was about to enter the tipi, Grandma called out to her from the RV.

"Bring your things over here, girl," she said. "I've got a bad back and painful arthritis. I don't sleep in a bedroll on the ground. You're staying with me here in my mobile home where the coffeemaker and microwave oven are."

Rhonda could barely believe her ears. But even though she felt a little guilty about abandoning the rest of the youth council, the girl happily headed for the motorized shelter.

"Are you sure?" she asked as she laid her things down on the floor of the RV.

"Absolutely," Grandma said. "You'll thank me later."

After getting a welcoming hug from the elder, Rhonda headed off to find the ground crew and begin another day in the encampment. Her mind danced with feelings of hope she had almost forgotten.

Over the next few days, life in the camp developed a steady rhythm. Cars, vans, and trucks filled with campers continued to roll in. New tents and tipis sprang up on the land that stretched from the Spirit Camp in the north to the reservation entrance sign to the south, and from the blacktop road on the east side to the river on the west side.

As Grandma had said, people of all colors, races, and ages poured into the area. The encampment became a little city, and campers were encouraged to stop by the HQ tent to sign up for various duties. In addition to kitchen and ground crew duties, you could sign up to be supply runners, sign makers, trash collectors, porta-potty sanitizers, day-care providers, food and clothing donation sorters, and a dozen other jobs.

Most people wanted to primarily serve as pipeline protestors, the main reason the camp existed, the main reason they were all there. But the whole objective would be undermined and turned into messy chaos unless everyone also took on these additional duties.

No traditional Native event or activity could succeed without a ceremonial or spiritual center. The encampment was founded with ceremony and continued to function with ceremony. Spiritual leaders from the Seven Fires of the Great Sioux Nation had supervised these ritual duties from the beginning. Their own Seven Fires Camp had been established just inside the Standing Stone reservation border near the highway.

Members of the seven tribes of Sioux people congregated and camped at or near the Seven Fires Camp, and their numbers were growing right along with the number of campers on Grandma Maxine's family land.

Just as the encampment had grown into a city, so had the ranks of demonstrators grown into an entire army of peaceful protesters. Daily, the pipeline workers watched as more and more people joined the protest and the single line developed into a dense crowd.

A Victory and a Warning

The very next morning, Rhonda awoke to the ground-shaking growls of mechanized earth-moving equipment. One by one, the bulldozers, dump trucks, and motorized ditchdiggers rumbled to life.

Peeking through a curtain in Grandma's RV, the teen saw the machines off in the distance taking up positions to resume their creation of the hated Black Snake. Quickly, Rhonda threw on some clothes and headed out of the RV. She intended to go next door to the Spirit Camp lodge but saw dozens of sign-carrying campers rushing northward toward the site of construction.

"What's the plan?" Rhonda asked Pam, who was coming out of the Spirit Camp lodge.

"Last night, the leaders of the Seven Fires Camp voted to lay down in front of the machinery when construction began again," Pam explained. "Many people volunteered to do that."

"That sounds so crazy and dangerous!" Rhonda exclaimed. "What are you going to do?"

"I still have my camp job, and so do you," Pam replied. "Now those jobs are more important than ever. We've got to keep the camp running as smoothly as possible so frontline people can do what they need to do."

Just then Grandma Little Moon stuck her head out of the RV and called out to Rhonda.

"Climb up on the roof of the RV and take selfies or chat-snaps or whatever you young people do," she said. "Post 'em on Spacebook or My Face or Twittergram—one of those."

Rhonda scanned the outside of the RV and found a ladder attached to the back of it.

"Great idea, Grandma!"

Rhonda raced up the ladder, reached the roof, and took in the view. About two hundred yards to the west of the blacktop road, protesters began lying down on the ground. Rhonda whipped out her phone and began recording. But she was too far from the action, and she couldn't clearly see what was happening, even when the lens was zoomed in all the way.

After she climbed down the ladder, Rhonda explained her problem to Grandma Maxine.

"We gotta get you closer," Grandma said, grabbing a set of keys attached to a beaded keychain. "Follow me."

Grandma led Rhonda around to the other side of the RV, where an aging red Ford Ranger pickup truck sat. A sticker in the back window read, "COLUMBUS WAS AN ILLEGAL ALIEN."

"Get in, and I'll drive you over there," Grandma said as she climbed into the driver's seat.

The engine roared to life as Rhonda climbed into the passenger side. Kicking up a cloud of dust, the pickup raced away from the RV. As they turned onto the gravel road, Rhonda could more clearly see what was unfolding ahead of them.

"Stop here!" Rhonda yelled as they reached the perfect place to film everything.

She jumped out of the passenger seat, climbed into the truck bed, and pulled out her phone. Steadying the phone's camera by resting her elbows on the cab of the truck, Rhonda began recording.

Row after row of people of all ages, colors, and sizes laid their bodies out directly in the path of the big equipment. Back near the machinery, a man wearing a hard hat and an orange vest raised his hand over his head and signaled the drivers to move forward. He must be the foreman, Rhonda thought.

Shifting gears, the massive machines with their gigantic tires inched toward the defenseless protesters. On the ground, the Water Protectors chanted in unison, "Water is life. We are life. We are the water!"

As the foreman continued to urge his drivers onward, and more people took up a place in their path, Rhonda's phone camera caught all of it.

When the lead bulldozer was within ten feet of the first line of protectors, the foreman signaled the driver to stop. Raising a powered megaphone to his mouth, he spoke to the people lined up on the ground.

"You are trespassing on federally restricted land," the man told them. "This project has received all the documentation required to continue construction. Unless you move out of the way now, you will be forcibly removed."

At that point, a Native man lying in the front row of protectors stood up and faced the fellow protectors. The large round patch on the back of his blue denim jacket said, "OIL SPOILS WATER." Putting a hand to the side of his mouth, he let loose a blood-curdling war cry maybe not heard since the days of his ancestor warriors of the plains. As if rehearsed, the entire body of protectors stood and stepped toward the line of big-wheeled construction equipment.

Soon the protectors began to chant, quietly at first and then louder and louder, "Native land, Native water. Native land, Native water. Native land, Native water." Over and over again the words rolled across the prairie. Soon the sound was almost deafening. When it was obvious that the protectors weren't about to move, the foreman signaled his drivers to turn around.

The chanting, however, continued until every last bulldozer, tractor, dump truck, and front-end loader was parked back where it was when the day began.

Then the Native man who began the chant raised his hand and signaled for the chant to end. The rolling hills immediately fell silent. The only sound to be heard was a gentle wind blowing across the prairie grass.

Then, triumphant yells of victory erupted from the army of protectors as they celebrated their successful attempt to stop the machinery. Rhonda jumped back into Grandma's truck.

"Can you take me to the generator truck?" she asked. "I need to post this as soon as possible."

"Hoka hey!" Grandma yelled as she turned the truck around. "You go, girl."

After the video was posted on multiple social media channels, Rhonda and Grandma walked to the camp's central ceremonial circle. Camp leaders had called for a meeting to discuss the morning's events.

Grandma sat on one of the tree stumps that had been placed in a circle around the fire pit. Rhonda stood behind her. The Native man who'd led the chant earlier stepped into the center of the circle.

"For those of you who don't know me, my name is Vernon White Bull, and I work with the Native Environmental Network," he said as he slowly rotated in a circle so everyone could hear him.

The circle of people erupted in applause, war cries, and ululations, as they were excited that this man and his family were with them.

"Of course, this morning's victory feels good," he continued. "You all did good, but I want you to prepare yourself for what's bound to come next."

The crowd quieted.

"I've seen this kind of thing before, and I don't want you to have any naive expectations about where this is going," he said. "The oil company *will* retaliate with an armed response."

The crowd grew even quieter.

"Maybe not tomorrow or the next day," he admonished, "but soon."

The mood in the camp was somber the rest of the day. Of course, all the campers, including Rhonda, carried out their duties as usual. But the seriousness and potential dangers of their actions seemed to sink in more than ever before.

Meanwhile, out in the cyber world, something spectacular was happening. Rhonda's video began to go viral. Native, environmental, and social justice organizations shared the startling images throughout their networks, and then the individual members of those groups did the same. Along the way, someone added the caption, "Showdown at Standing Stone" to the front of the video.

By nightfall, the video had found its way to local, regional, and national news outlets, appearing on television, cell phone, and tablet screens all over the country.

Breaking News

Over the next few days, nervous water protectors showed up at the front line each morning with signs, banners, and protest chants ready to take on whatever response might be coming. To the west, pipeline workers also showed up each morning, expecting to start their equipment and move the pipeline further eastward. But nothing happened. Well, not exactly nothing.

More caravans of cars, trucks, vans, and SUVs streamed into the camping areas. With them also came bloggers, vloggers, reporters, and photographers. In turn, a steady flow of news reports, interviews with protest organizers, and images of the growing camp began streaming out to the rest of the nation and the world.

Rhonda was busier than ever with Billy and the ground crew, directing newcomers to designated camping spaces, helping set up their camps, and doing every logistical and maintenance job imaginable.

And not only had her video gone viral on the web, but also word of who shot the video went viral throughout the camp. Rhonda, unexpectedly, became sort of a folk hero to everyone involved with the protests. Her mode of remaining the invisible girl who blended in with the background vanished. Thrust into the camp spotlight, her levels of anxiety began to rise, and her need to retreat from view spiked. At a time when others might have welcomed the attention, she shrank from it.

By lunchtime on the fifth day of her unwelcome fame, Rhonda had to hide. When folks began asking Grandma where Rhonda had gone, the elder returned to the RV. There, cowering under a Pendleton blanket, was Rhonda.

"Don't like the attention, huh?" Grandma said as she sat on the edge of Rhonda's fold-out bed.

Rhonda merely shook her head.

"I bet you're feeling nervous and agitated," the elder said.

Rhonda nodded.

"After your suicide attempt, I bet you got a prescription for anxiety medication, didn't you?"

Rhonda sat up, realizing something.

"I ran out of the pills a few days ago," she said. "But I've been so busy here, I forgot to do anything about it."

"Let me take you to the tribal clinic on the rez so you can get a refill," Grandma offered. "You've made amazing progress in your recovery, and I'd hate for you to suffer a setback now."

"How do you know so much about me?" Rhonda asked as she slipped out from under the blanket. "I feel like you can read my mind or something."

"Haven't you heard?" she replied with a smile. "I'm a wise Indian elder!"

The gleam in the elder's eyes let Rhonda know Grandma was kidding, but the teen knew it was really true.

"In my long years of life, Creator has gifted me with insights, and living on the rez has shown me plenty of pain," the elder continued. "I know it when I see it in our people's eyes."

Grandma drove Rhonda to the nearest tribal clinic about thirty miles away. While the girl talked to a doctor and got a new supply of medication, the elder spoke to the clinic's director about the need for emergency medical personnel out at the camp.

"Tribal Chairman Smoke said we should be on call and ready to go in case people suffer injuries during the protests," the director, a pale man wearing black-rimmed glasses, said. "We told him we could be out there within two or three hours."

"That's not good enough," the elder replied. "You need to have a couple of ambulances and medics on-site, because there *will* be injuries in need of immediate treatment within the next two days!"

"I'll have to clear that with my boss at the Indian Health Service," the director said nervously.

"Well, you do that," she replied politely. "But I'm chairwoman of the Standing Stone Elders Committee, and we'll be calling for your resignation if you don't have those vehicles and techs stationed at the camp by tomorrow morning!"

Grandma left the man speechless in his office as she met up with Rhonda who, with medication in hand, was ready to head back to camp.

When the elder and the teen awoke the following morning, two ambulances and four medical technicians had set up a medical tent not far from the HQ tent. Mission accomplished, Grandma thought.

It was a good thing, too, because the very next morning, uniformed men and women wearing protective vests and carrying nightsticks greeted the protectors when they arrived at the front line. Were these law enforcement officers from nearby agencies? None of the Water Protectors could tell for sure, but patches on uniforms contained only the word "ProForce." An added threatening element accompanying the humans was a contingent of twelve trained dogs. With teeth bared, the animals strained against leashes held by a dozen of the uniformed people.

Grandma and Rhonda positioned themselves nearby, as they'd done the last time there was a confrontation. What was different this time was that a dozen other people with various kinds of cameras had already taken up positions at strategic vantage points to capture the action. Some were streaming live online. As they filmed, events began to unfold.

Led by Vernon White Bull again, the protectors lined up shoulder to shoulder facing the dogs and their keepers. At the signal from their leader, the protesters simultaneously raised their hands in the air as if they were under arrest. This showed they were unarmed and nonviolent.

At that point several of the guards pulled out cans of pepper spray. The guards with spray cans and the guards with dogs moved toward the protectors at the same time. Egged on by their keepers, the dogs strained harder against their leashes and barked ferociously at the protectors. Cameras continued to record and stream.

As the front row of protectors got pepper sprayed, they covered their faces and eyes. Unable to see, they were easy prey for the attack dogs that began clawing and biting them. Some protectors screamed and ran for their lives. Others fell to their knees in place and cowered in the fetal position with their knees tucked under their chins.

After the protectors began to scatter, the guards turned their attention toward the people on the fringes who were recording the event. Running alongside their dogs, these guards pursued anyone with a phone or camera. One pair charged toward Grandma's truck, where Rhonda was again recording the action.

"Hold on to something!" Grandma yelled out the truck window. Rhonda squatted in the truck bed as the elder put the gear in reverse and sped backward down the gravel road. The guard and his dog turned toward another target. Hitting the brake pedal hard, Grandma put the truck into a spinning, sliding stop on the gravel surface. When the dust settled a little, Rhonda could see that they were now facing forward toward the camp.

"Get in!" the elder yelled to her passenger.

Rhonda jumped out of the truck bed and into the cab. Grandma put the pedal to the metal and steered for the medical tent. In no particular hurry, the medics were loading medical supplies into their ambulances.

"What's the matter with you?" Grandma demanded. "Get your butts in gear and get out there. We got people blinded by pepper spray and bitten by vicious dogs!"

Hearing this, the medics sprang into action. Quickly loading the rest of their supplies, they flipped on their sirens and raced toward the wounded campers. The guards and their dogs withdrew when they heard the sirens. Arriving on the scene within minutes, the medics were able to quickly treat the injured while cameras clicked and video was recorded.

By that evening, images of the morning's violent attack on defenseless protestors reached every corner of America. Everyone from government officials to legitimate law enforcement agencies denounced the events. Quick investigations revealed that the oil company had hired the ProForce private security company to deal with protestors. Politicians, mostly concerned with their public image, strenuously called for further investigations.

The oil company, concerned with their own public image, tried to make apologies for the "unfortunate circumstances in which they found themselves." They decided to pause their construction efforts for the time being to see what their options were for future action.

However, the sheriff of the county where all this was taking place issued a media statement calling the protestors terrorists and blaming them for what he called an "unlawful riot." He said the guards were attacked by protestors wielding posts and flagpoles and any such action in the future would result in arrests and jail time.

None of that mattered to the thousands of people outraged and motivated by images of the attack dogs and pepper spray. Day after day, protest supporters streamed into the overflowing camps. Many set up tents right in the pipeline's designated path, on both sides of the river.

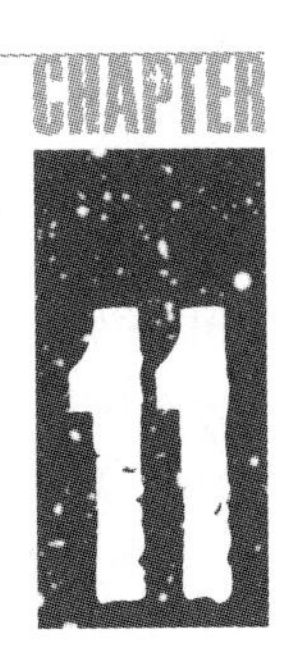

Tasers, Batons, and Rubber Bullets

By midsummer, the little tent city grew to a medium-size tent city as the number of protest campers grew to around four thousand. And when Rhonda's eighteenth birthday rolled around on July 15, thousands of people were ready to celebrate their local folk hero, including her uncle Floyd.

"I've been following you on Facebook," he said when the teen answered her ringing phone. "Quite a mind-expanding experience you seem to be having over there. I guess you aren't missing us back here at Blackfeet."

"My best friend is dead, and my other friends are kind of lame," she replied flatly. "My mother's in prison, and my grandmother is a total witch. So, what's to miss?"

Floyd didn't answer.

"Oh, and of course there's you, who I completely miss every single day!" she said. You could hear the smile in her voice, she was so happy to hear from him.

"Whew, I'm glad to hear that," Floyd answered. "You had me worried there for a minute."

"This *is* a mind-expanding experience, and I'm totally into it," she said. "Things I learned from you I put to use all the time."

"Well, happy birthday, Miss Eighteen-year-old," he said. "I really mean that, because you deserve to be happy today and the rest of your life."

Floyd wrapped up the call with a promise to keep following his niece online.

All that day, campers stopped by the RV to drop off various kinds of food they had cooked on their camp stoves or dug out of their ice chests—lopsided cupcakes, large and small cookies, cans of soda, strange-looking salads, hot dogs, sandwiches, vegan dishes—whatever they could manage.

As practical and giving as ever, Grandma suggested they invite the nearest campers to a little birthday party that evening so the teen could share all that food. Of course, nearby campers spread word of the party to campers a little farther away, and on and on it went.

At the appointed hour, Rhonda and Grandma stepped out of the RV to be greeted by the happy faces of hundreds of people spread out down the hillside from the Spirit Camp.

Rhonda had never seen anything like it. Her first impulse, of course, was to run and hide. But Grandma and the youth council convinced Rhonda that she deserved the praise and attention that was coming her way, so she reluctantly accepted it. The girl who wanted to remain invisible was now semi-famous.

By summer's end, the medium-size tent city grew to a large tent city, boasting at least eight thousand residents. Campsites lined both sides of the river and also filled several hundred feet of the pipeline easement. This worried Grandma because she knew those people were trespassing on property controlled by the Army Corps of Engineers, the federal agency monitoring the pipeline project.

Meanwhile, the pipeline construction was being delayed. The oil company and the tribe legally fought each other in front of state and federal judges, as each side attempted to have the conflict settled in the courts once and for all.

Back at the camp, movie stars and politicians began arriving to show their support for the protest. The entertainment reporters and political journalists who followed these celebrities fed news stories and images of these appearances to the national media, keeping the protest in the national spotlight.

As summer gave way to autumn, Rhonda spent less of her time with the ground crew and more of her time in the main HQ tent, the Spirit Camp lodge, and the central lodges of the other camps. During Labor Day weekend, Pam left the camp to begin her life as a college student.

Before leaving, Pam had some encouraging words for the Blackfeet teen.

"You catch on to things so fast," Pam said. "And your ability to size up a situation and quickly take action is amazing."

"You and my uncle are good teachers," Rhonda replied modestly. "No big deal."

"It is a big deal, so I hope you'll think about stepping into my shoes when I'm gone," Pam said.

The thought hadn't entered Rhonda's mind, so she talked about it with Grandma later.

"Go for it," the elder quickly said. "There's nobody better suited for the job than you. And if you need guidance, I'm here for you."

"Go for it," Rhonda said more to herself than to Grandma. "If I think about it too long I'll talk myself out of it. So here I go."

Immediately, she walked over to the HQ tent and boldly presented herself as Pam's replacement.

She was surprised to find that Pam had already given her a ringing endorsement. With no hesitation, the camp's leadership committee gave Rhonda the job, along with a new walkie-talkie, a clipboard with camp duties that needed to be filled, and a pat on the back.

During this same time, camp populations grew even larger, drawn by the continual flow of media coverage. However, Grandma, who regularly surveyed the camp from the cab of her red Ranger, noticed a disturbing pattern emerging.

From Grandma's point of view, it seemed that news broadcasts often focused on the conflict and drama of the protests. People angered by what they'd seen online and on TV arrived at the camp driven by that anger. And many of those same people ended up on the fringes of the original encampment, out of reach of the already overworked and understaffed camp volunteers. So they never heard the important message of keeping the protests peaceful, nonviolent, and well coordinated.

Being famous was the goal of some of these protesters, Grandma thought, as they pulled what could only be called publicity stunts. They made sure a camera recorded their actions as they chained themselves to bulldozers or front-end loaders. Others punctured the tires of oil company trucks or vandalized the construction equipment in some very visible way.

These actions drew multiple law enforcement agencies to the pipeline construction site. Local and state police, accompanied by National Guardsmen, arrived at the scene dressed in riot gear. Carrying assault rifles, these forces came to clear the pipeline's path of protestors and their camps.

Rhonda and Grandma watched in horror as these forces, using an assortment of Tasers, rubber bullets, and clubs, created an impenetrable moving wall to evict people from the construction zone. Dozens of unarmed people were injured by the action. More than one hundred and thirty were arrested, their tents torn down, and their personal belongings thrown into dumpsters.

Reporters and videographers recording the episode were also targeted in the sweep. As directed by the local county sheriff, some were arrested just for being there with their cameras on. He justified this action later by noting they were trespassing on land under the control of the Army Corps of Engineers.

With each of these incidents of violence, Rhonda felt increasingly alarmed and personally threatened, even though she wasn't among the frontline protectors. With the help of Grandma, the Spirit Camp youth, and the increased participation in Native ceremonies, the teen began to realize that her own self-protective barriers were coming down. A feeling of connectedness had been growing within her, dispelling much of the darkness that had lurked in the corners of her soul.

While this sense of openness had helped her feel more alive, it also increased the feeling that she was surrounded by, and more vulnerable to, increasing danger. Again, with Grandma's input, which was every bit as effective as any therapist's guidance, Rhonda's outlook on life was definitely more open and positive than it had ever been.

As November replaced October on the calendar, colder winds began to sweep across the plains. Seeing that winter was on its way, some people realized they were really only fair-weather protesters and headed for home. Many others, however, who'd come from nearby northern states, were ready to face the coming colder weather with blankets, heavy coats, wood-burning heaters, and winter-worthy camping gear.

Responding to Grandma's invitation, a gathering of several hundred religious leaders from all over North America came in early November to join the protectors in a day of prayer and ceremony, hoping to end the violence and stop the pipeline. By that time, representatives from more than one hundred tribal nations had also made their way to the camp, and their flags were added to those already on-site. Viewed from a distance, the brown autumn grasses along the river seemed to burst with brilliant spring colors that danced in the wind.

In spite of the thousands of prayers and months of ceremony, word came down to the camp's HQ in mid-November that all legal options for stopping the pipeline had been pursued and exhausted. Corporate and government entities seemed to have successfully merged their forces to deny every petition, motion, or legal action the tribes and environmental groups could muster.

The Thanksgiving holiday arrived to find a disheartened army of protectors experiencing daytime temperatures in the midthirties and nighttime temperatures dipping into the upper teens.

Of course, for many Natives, Thanksgiving was observed as a National Day of Mourning, not a time of joy and celebration. Rhonda learned from Grandma that the idea that the Pilgrims and Indians of the Northeast sat down to a bountiful feast enjoyed by immigrants and indigenous peoples alike was a myth begun in the era of Abraham Lincoln.

On the Monday after Thanksgiving, Rhonda got word that pipeline workers would be returning to their machines, accompanied by a full contingent of military might. Cleared by the courts to proceed, the oil company had a green light to move dirt and push people out of the way. Truckloads of National Guardsmen lined up in front of the big-wheeled, heavy equipment. A whistle blew, and the expulsion of protectors began.

In the most brutal show of force to date, campsites in the pipeline's path were crushed. Any person found in those sites who wasn't readily evacuating was seized, arrested, and escorted to waiting prison buses. Protectors from the main camp watched in horror as the chaos unfolded before them. Tribal leaders urged them to refrain from engaging in the conflict.

Rhonda and her phone camera witnessed the entire process from atop Grandma's RV, as the heavy equipment and military force pushed eastward almost to the river. Tears streamed down the girl's face as months of bottled-up fear and tension were released in a flow of sheer emotional agony. Feeling faint, Grandma escaped to the RV, where she proceeded to crash on her bed and cover her head with a blanket, as Rhonda had done before.

Distraught beyond belief, Rhonda kept it together long enough to make it to the generator truck to email the new video to her uncle Floyd and share it on social media.

What Do We Do Now?

The following day, Chairman Smoke paid a visit to the camp. Disillusioned protectors gathered around the camp's central ceremonial circle wearing heavy coats or wrapped in blankets. A warming fire burned in the fire pit, but everyone's breath was visible in the cold morning air.

"It's clear we've lost this battle," the chairman said with a sad expression on his face. "We thank you for your sacrifice and your valiant efforts, but I'm afraid it's time to go home."

A general grumbling spread through the shivering crowd.

"I know this is a big disappointment," he continued. "We all feel that way, but there's no reason for you all to stay on and face the brutal winter weather."

With that, the man turned and walked away. No one moved as they watched him drive away in his black truck with the Standing Stone tribal seal on the door. Rhonda was standing with her friends from the International Council of Native Youth, and they began talking among themselves about this news.

"What are we going to do?" one girl asked the others in the group. "You guys are like my family now, and there's nothing for me back home on my rez."

"Donations have come in from all over the country to support our efforts," another one responded. "I think people expect us to carry on with the fight somehow."

"We're staying on Grandma's land, not the reservation's or the federal government's," Rhonda said. "Maybe we should ask her about what she wants to do."

They walked up the hill to the Spirit Camp lodge, where a fire burned inside. They gathered around the fire while Rhonda went to the RV to talk to Grandma. Soon the two returned.

"I'm not moving the RV or taking down the lodge anytime soon," Grandma told them. "This is my family's land, and you can stay as long as you want. You young people are our best hope for a positive future, and I'll support you anyway I can."

That, of course, was good news for members of the ICNY, who now felt they at least had some time to decide their collective future. But the camp population did begin to dwindle a little as people considered the chairman's words, and a few chose to head home.

What surprised everyone who stayed behind was the arrival of hundreds and then thousands of military veterans from all parts of the United States during the first days of December. Within a few days, four thousand veterans had come to the area to participate in the protest, many staying in nearby hotels and motels. The whole thing had been organized by a handful of men and women who had defended the nation but now believed leaders of the country had taken a wrong turn regarding the environment, the wars in the Middle East, and the harsh treatment of Native protesters.

Rhonda was surprised to see that her uncle Floyd was among the veterans who'd come to "Stand with Standing Stone," as the veterans' campaign was called. As soon as the man set foot on the campgrounds, he asked where he could find his niece. Everyone pointed up the hill toward the Spirit Camp lodge.

There Floyd found her, encircled by the youth council as they planned their next moves. The delighted surprise he saw on his niece's face made the whole ice-cold, snow-covered trip worthwhile. But their initial reunion was brief because the time had come for the veterans to execute their pre-planned action.

Floyd explained to Rhonda that the purpose of their visit to the camp was not to confront pipeline workers or police. The purpose was to bring the nation's attention to an important moment in the country's history. On the morning of December fifth, General George Armstrong Custer's birthday, their purpose was to have former enemies unite in one cause. Descendants of those who fought against one another in the Indian Wars of the 1800s would now stand together in solidarity to protect Mother Earth.

The powerful and symbolic union took place as military veterans and elders of the Great Sioux Nation marched and stood together on a bridge that overlooked the path of the destructive Black Snake. Prayers were offered and words were spoken that helped to mend the broken hearts of veterans and Natives alike.

In spite of frozen fingers and toes, Rhonda and others filmed the whole inspiring event, which lifted the spirits of protectors who felt defeated. The overall effect of the veterans' visit was to validate the ICNY's belief that there was still plenty of support in the country for their goal to continue their mission.

What would happen next took Grandma, the youth, and all the remaining protectors completely by surprise.

The Final Blow

As the veterans were saying their goodbyes and heading for home, the winter's first blizzard began to blow into the camp. For several hours, wind-driven wet snow fell at a sharp angle against the tents and tipis still standing on the land just south of the Black Snake's trail.

Using fifty-five–gallon steel barrels, many campers lit fires to provide warming stations around the camp. The youth near the Spirit Camp lodge did the same, but also had the lodge's interior fire going.

Because of the intense cold, the youth had invited elders from the camp to join them in the warmth of the youth lodge for the day. As Natives had done in winter months for centuries, elders took turns telling ancient stories to pass on wisdom to the younger generation. Gallons of hot chocolate, herbal tea, and campfire coffee were consumed as the stories and the warm feelings flowed.

It was around noon when Rhonda heard the rumblings of heavy vehicles. From inside the lodge, it sounded like army tanks were moving down the blacktop road that ran beside Grandma's land and the rest of the camp.

Rhonda opened the east-facing flap of the lodge and stepped out to see what was up. The blizzard, thankfully, had eased up. As she rounded the tipi to get a better look at what was making all the racket on the road, she got the shock of her life. A line of dozens of army-green fire trucks and armored personnel carriers were moving into position on the blacktop.

Rhonda ran back into the lodge and alerted everyone about what she'd seen. She reached for her walkie-talkie radio and was about to push the talk button when she heard it crackle to life.

"HQ to all members of the ground crew and logistics team," a voice on the radio said. "Be advised that militarized police units have just shown up on our doorstep, arriving in heavily armored vehicles. We don't know their intent, but do not confront them. Tell all those around you, do not engage."

People who'd been standing near the barrel fires scampered toward their tents or their cars parked nearby. For a long moment, all was still. No one or nothing moved. After a time, when nothing bad happened, people began to venture out to see what was going on.

That's when it hit. Powerful water cannons began shooting jets of pressurized water from some of the trucks. Anyone standing within range was swept off their feet, drenched with freezing water, and washed toward the river. Smaller tents nearby, as well as camping gear, collapsed into soggy heaps on the frozen ground.

Then, poncho-draped police officers stepped from behind the trucks waving their batons. In a repeat of the previous fall's violent actions, these men swept through the camp, intent on the eviction of every man, woman, and child from the premises.

Hearing screams of pain and sounds of water cannons shredding tents, Rhonda peeked out of the lodge again. Witnessing what was an incomprehensible site, she quickly ducked back inside. With only a moment's thought and no hesitation, the girl immediately got everyone in the Spirit Camp lodge organized.

"Elders, move quickly to the center of the lodge near the fire," she ordered. "ICNY, form a circle around them."

"What the hell's going on?" Grandma demanded of no one in particular. "They can't force me off my own land!"

"They can and they will," Rhonda replied to the elder, and then to the youth she said, "Face outward and lock arms. We'll form a human shield around our elders."

Panicked, members of the ICNY didn't move. Did they hear Rhonda right?

"We've got about ten seconds!" Rhonda yelled. "Are you with me or not? Are we going to live up to our promises or not?"

With a look of resolve, the youth stepped one by one into the circle, faced outward from the elders, and locked arms with their neighbor. Each of them realized full well that he or she might be injured for making this stand.

Moments later, half a dozen uniformed men stepped into the tipi.

"Vacate the premises now or you will be arrested!" the man in front barked.

Rhonda and the youth braced themselves, locking arms even more tightly.

From within the circle of elders, Grandma stood up and shouted, "You can't evict us. This is my property, and these people are here as my guests."

"So you say, old lady!" the man in charge fired back. "Okay men, move in."

Forming a semicircle, the officers approached the outer circle of youth. On a signal from their commander, they grabbed the arms, elbows, or wrists of the nearest young person.

Rhonda yelled to her cohorts, "Remember what the elders taught us! Resist, but don't fight back!"

Not achieving the desired result using only their hands, the men reached for the batons that hung from their utility belts. The circle of youth cowered a little at the thought of being struck with the batons but managed to hold their positions. Rather than striking them, the men used the sticks as leverage to pry their arms apart. A couple of the youth cried out in pain.

Suddenly Rhonda heard the snap of bone breaking followed by the loudest cry of all. Turning to look behind her, the Blackfeet teen saw the youngest, smallest girl among them collapse on the ground holding her noticeably bent forearm.

"Enough!" Grandma yelled. "Enough!"

The officers froze in place, waiting for further command.

"Rhonda, what you're trying to do here is good, but I'm not willing to risk any more pain and suffering," Grandma said.

Still standing with locked arms, the teen turned to look at the elder.

Grandma smiled back at the girl and said, "It's okay. We'll go quietly."

The youth released their grip on one another, feeling as though they'd failed their elders and failed in their mission. The youth on either side of the injured teen turned to help her.

Sensing the emotions of the young people, Grandma stepped toward the policemen and said, "Our warriors of old would be so proud of you young people today. You stood your ground, ready to give your lives for us. No one could ask for anything more."

With that, Grandma held her arms together out in front waiting for handcuffs to be slapped on them. The commanding officer merely grabbed the elder by one arm and led her away. Other officers showed up to escort everyone in the lodge to waiting personnel carriers.

When the group arrived at the sheriff's office, a waiting ambulance took the injured teen to the hospital. As for the rest, each one was booked and fingerprinted. As the commander fingerprinted Grandma, she quipped, "Not my first time in jail, sonny. Ain't no big deal."

Then she winked at Rhonda before wiping the ink from her fingers. The officer tried to rush her away, but the elder pulled herself loose from his grip. Standing taller and straighter than before, she smoothed a few wrinkles in her dress. When she was all done, she indicated to the man that she was ready to go to her cell.

Taking her cue from Grandma, Rhonda also displayed the attitude that this was no big deal. All part of a day's work as a Native activist. And her first night in lockup really wasn't going to be all that bad. It beat spending the night out at the camp in freezing overnight temperatures and twenty-five-mile-an-hour winds.

Water Protector Forever

The following morning, Standing Stone tribal attorneys paid bail and got the elders and the youth released from jail. In the process, the Native lawyers were quick to let the sheriff know they would be taking him and his officers to court for trespassing on private property, police brutality, and wrongful arrest.

The sheriff claimed he was only following orders from the state governor's office and didn't realize most of the encampment they just raided was on private land. His office had been informed incorrectly that the camp was on pipeline land and had to be cleared of protesters.

"Likely story," Grandma said as she and Rhonda left the jail.

A van belonging to the tribe drove the elder and the teen back to Grandma's RV. As the pair stepped out of the van, they were shocked by what they saw. Grotesque ice sculptures were scattered across the landscape from the blacktop road to the river.

Actually, these were the remnants of collapsed tents, tipis, and a variety of camping equipment that had been frozen in place overnight after being sprayed by the water cannons. Grandma's large tipi, the Spirit Camp lodge, had suffered the same fate, looking very much like the broken mast and sail of a sailboat locked in ice at the North Pole.

Fortunately, the large, sturdy RV survived the aquatic attack with no damage, so Grandma and Rhonda climbed aboard.

"I guess it's all over, and the whole thing was for nothing," Rhonda said with obvious disappointment. "I can add it to the list of failures in my life."

"Oh, child, you're so very wrong about that," the elder said as she sat down at the RV's built-in dining table. "It wasn't for nothing, it's far from over, and failure is not an option."

Rhonda let that sink in as she rummaged through the kitchen cabinets looking for something to eat. After finding a box of packaged cheese and crackers, she sat down across from the elder. Grandma could tell she was thinking hard about something as the girl ripped open the package and began munching.

"Sure, these guys are going to build their pipeline under this river," the elder said. "But already there are a half dozen other oil pipelines being planned in Canada and here in the States that could pollute Native lands and waterways."

With a shocked look on her face, Rhonda stopped chewing the mouthful of food she had been working on.

"You mean there could be more of these Black Snakes slithering around?" she said, almost choking. She got a glass of water, filled it, and washed the bite down.

"Yes, I'm afraid so," Grandma replied. "But you know what we have now that we didn't have before?"

"What's that?" Rhonda asked.

"An experienced young leader who knows how to plan and coordinate opposition to environmental injustices and an army of motivated people willing to carry out those plans," the elder said.

"Oh yeah, and just who is that young leader you're talking about?" the teen asked as she took another gulp of water.

"You, silly," came the response.

Totally surprised by that reply, Rhonda almost choked on the water.

"Me? What do I know about it?"

"Child, come over here and give me your hand," Grandma requested, echoing the words she spoke to the girl when they first met.

As Rhonda put out her hand and the elder took it, that feeling of warm energy enveloped the girl, that same feeling she felt at their first meeting.

"You are no longer that depressed girl with no future who tried to take her own life all those months ago," Grandma said in a quiet, gentle voice. "You are a whole new person, and I watched as you became that whole new person."

Rhonda's eyes began to tear up as the elder continued.

"That new person has seen and felt the worst the world could throw at her," the elder said. "That new person has gained new knowledge and felt a new connection to the earth and other people. And that new person didn't hesitate to use her own body to shield defenseless elders against a violent force. That new person is a Water Protector forever."

Tears trickled down Rhonda's cheeks as she felt acceptance she'd never experienced before. But that feeling was interrupted by another thought, and the girl withdrew her hand from the elder's. Reaching for a paper towel hanging from a rack under the nearby kitchen cabinet, the teen dried her eyes.

"You have more confidence in me than I have in myself," Rhonda said. "But there's one little problem I've got to face."

"What's that?" Grandma asked, even though she already knew what the girl was going to say.

"I am pretty much homeless right now, so where would I plan and coordinate this opposition from?"

Again, echoing her first words to Rhonda, Grandma said, "If you wouldn't mind keeping an old lady company, I'd like to invite you stay with me at my house on the rez for as long as you like."

Rhonda was speechless.

"You could operate the headquarters of the International Council of Native Youth from there, you know, and reach out to other Native youth."

Rhonda still couldn't speak.

"And you could carry on your work as a Water Protector from there too."

Rhonda was overwhelmed by the generosity of Grandma's invitation, her unconditional acceptance, and the confidence the elder had in her.

"Water Protector," Rhonda repeated out loud. "I like the sound of that. If someone asks what I do, I can say I'm a Water Protector. That's my job title, my mission in life. I am a Water Protector forever."

With excitement in her voice, Rhonda sat down at the RV dining table and began recording Water Protector ideas, plans, and to-do lists on her smartphone. At that moment, Grandma knew the future of Native communities would be in good hands.

RESOURCES

To find out more or to get involved with the real-life Water Protectors or with Native American environmental protection, contact the following organizations:

Indigenous Environmental Network:

ienearth.org

The International Indigenous Youth Council:

indigenousyouth.org

Water Protector Legal Collective:

waterprotectorlegal.org

To find out more about Native American suicides or to contact someone who can help with suicide prevention, contact the following resources:

National Suicide Prevention Lifeline:

1-800-273-8255

MentalHealth.gov/what-to-look-for/suicidal-behavior

The Indian Health Service Suicide Prevention Programs:

ihs.gov/suicideprevention

The U.S. Department of Health and Human Services Substance Abuse and Mental Health Services Administration:

samhsa.gov/tribal-ttac/resources/suicide-prevention

ABOUT THE AUTHOR

GARY ROBINSON is an award-winning writer and filmmaker of Choctaw and Cherokee descent. He has participated in the production of over one hundred Native American educational and informational television projects documenting the history, culture, and contemporary issues of indigenous peoples. His passions include writing books, making videos, and creating digital content and multimedia stories that bust stereotypes, correct misinformation, and dispel myths about American Indians. For more information, visit his website at tribaleyeproductions.com.

PathFinders novels offer exciting contemporary and historical stories featuring Native teens and written by Native authors. For more information, visit: NativeVoicesBooks.com

Trust Your Name
Tim Tingle
978-1-939053-19-0 • $9.95

Nowhere to Hide
Kim Sigafus
978-1-939053-21-3 • $9.95

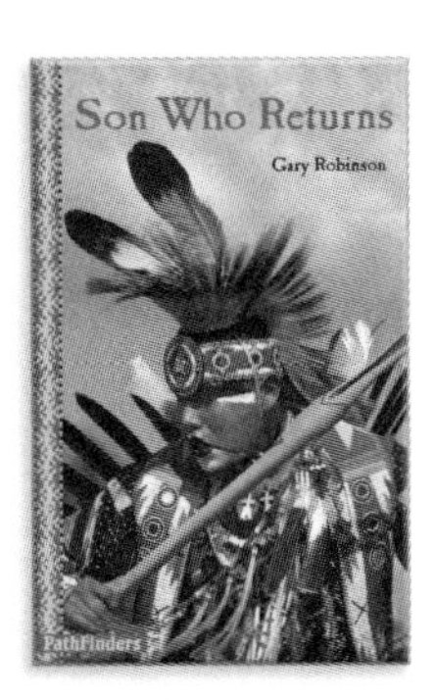

Son Who Returns
Gary Robinson
978-1-939053-04-6 • $9.95

Abnormal
Gary Robinson
978-1-939053-07-7 • $9.95

Available from your local bookstore or directly from:

Book Publishing Company • PO Box 99 • Summertown, TN 38483 • 888-260-8458

Free shipping and handling on all book orders